Testing *Tessa*

Healing the Wounded Heart series

Book 1

By Donna Schlachter

(c) 2020

ISBN: 978-1-943688-76-0

Published by: PLS Bookworks, Denver, Colorado

Where Publishing Dreams Become Reality

Note from the Author

NOTE: This book previously published in August 2020 as part of the "Nursing the Heart" series under the title *A Nurse for Caleb.*

All characters are from my imagination. Also from my imagination, although not entirely without foundation, is the possibility of the Colonies hiring a nurse. They often hired laborers and craftspeople from outside the Colonies, providing them with a permit house, three meals and snacks per day, plus a wage.

The Harrow School of Nursing is fictitious. However, while official schools for nurses began in the US in 1871, short courses such as the one mentioned in this book and the series were developed by Dr. Elizabeth Blackwell beginning in 1861, so nurses were completing training.

The Female Medical College of Pennsylvania did exist at the time, and a cholera epidemic went through Pennsylvania in 1866, brought on by contaminated water.

References to medical journals and medical textbooks, and to Dr. Henry Salter and Dr. Lister are factual. Understood causes of the day for asthma, and remedies for asthma and other ailments are drawn from medical texts of the day. *On Asthma: Its Pathology and Treatment* by Dr. Henry Salter is a well-known text.

All scripture references are from the King James Version of the Holy Bible (KJV)

Kind things folks are saying about

Testing *Tessa*

"If you enjoy Amish books, you'll fall in love with Donna Schlachter's, *A Nurse For Caleb.*

The novella is set in Homestead, Iowa in the Amana Sect, a German religious group that permits no outsiders, and lives in a communal style with communal dining, communal work, and communal church attendance. The group obeys strict rules that provide peace and continuity for their group.

Introduce into this peaceful setting an attempted murder and child abuse and you have a riveting story you won't be able to put down. Ms. Schlachter adds authentic touches about home nursing and life inside the group that add color and texture to her story. I'm sure you will love this charming novella." *Anne Greene, author of* Trial of Tears, Red Is For Rookie, Angel With Steel Wings, *and twenty-three other books.*

"Gifted author Donna Schlachter has woven memorable characters with superb storytelling. She captured the sights, sounds, smells, and spirit of a closed community of believers as well as the evil that lies in the heart of the antagonist. I was moved by the characters' struggles and successes and a touching story that will move your heart." *Susan G Mathis, author of* Devyn's Dilemma *and more.*

Books By Leeann Betts:

By the Numbers series featuring Carly Turnquist, forensic accountant

No Accounting for Murder
There Was a Crooked Man
Unbalanced
Five and Twenty Blackbirds
Broke, Busted, and Disgusted
Hidden Assets
Petty Cash
A Deadly Dissolution
Silent Partner
In the Money
Missing Deposits
Risk Management

Mysterious Ink Bookstore series featuring Margie Hanson, librarian

The Game is Afoot
Little Grey Cells

Counting the Days: a 31-day devotional
In Search of Christmas Past – a novel

Always a Wedding Planner Romance Collection
(Barbour Publishing June 2021)

By Leeann and Donna:

Nuggets of Writing Gold -- articles and essays on writing.

More Nuggets of Writing Gold – more articles and essays on writing

Books by Donna Schlachter:

***Mended by God* series – bringing healing and wholeness to your heart and soul**

Broken Dreams, Mended Heart
Broken Dreams, Mended Family
Broken Dreams, Mended Marriage

I Do – Again: a devotional for remarrieds

Second Chances and Second Cups: A short story collection.
The Physics of Love
The Mystery of Christmas Inn, Colorado
Christmas Under the Stars
Transformation – a devotional

***The Oregon Trail Mysteries* series**

Kate
A Pink Lady Thanksgiving

Trust in the Lord with all thine heart;

And lean not unto thine own understanding.

In all thy ways acknowledge Him,

And He shall direct thy paths.

Proverbs 3:5-6

Acknowledgements

First and foremost, to God the Father, God the Son,
and God the Holy Spirit. The triune Three in One.
Without Him, no story is worth telling.

To my husband, Patrick. My biggest fan and
the love of my life

Chapter 1

Tessa Mayer looked up from the medical textbook in her lap when the conductor entered their carriage. The kindly gentleman had kept her furnished with hot tea and an extra blanket throughout her three-day ordeal from Baltimore to her new home, miraculously changing trains with her in Chicago.

Goodness, had it been but four days since her graduation ceremony on September the third? Seemed like a month ago. At least.

"Homestead, Iowa, next stop. Homestead coming up."

She marked her page and closed the book, then looked around. A portly gentleman, sound asleep and pressing against her left arm, effectively pinned her into her seat. Several times in the past hour, his snoring filled her ear. And once, had it not been for the dear conductor who went by the name of Brand—whether first or last name she

9

didn't know—the stranger's head would have rested on her shoulder.

What would Miss Harrow think?

Likely not much more than the nursing school's founder already thought of her most peculiar student. Choosing an Old Order community wasn't her only unique trait.

Brand appeared at her side, his hand extended. "Can I take that heavy book for you, Miss Mayer?"

Tessa relinquished the volume. "Thank you." She glanced at her seatmate. "I don't suppose—"

"Not a problem, Miss." The conductor shook the man awake. "Are you getting off at Homestead, sir? Only we don't want you to miss your stop."

The passenger blinked a couple of times then straightened. "No, but is it your destination?"

Tessa nodded. "Thank you. I'd like a moment to gather my things." She stood, gripping the rail that held her traveling case overhead. "Why don't you slide over, then I'll be on the outside so I won't disturb you again."

The stranger did as suggested, nodded to both her and Brand, then leaned his head against the window and fell back to sleep, as his snoring confirmed.

Brand smiled at her again, the wrinkles framing his mouth and eyes as though much accustomed to being there. "I believe the lavatory is available, Miss. We'll be in Homestead in about ten minutes."

After a quick trip to wipe the dust from her face,

10

re-pin her hair, and damp-iron the front of her traveling dress, she returned to her seat and packed her book safely in her valise. An invaluable source of information, the expensive gift from her mentor was a cherished possession, one she was certain would assist her with her duties as nurse to the Amana Colonies.

She sat, the bag at her feet, as the train slowed and she caught her first glimpse of her new home.

Oh, dear. It was nothing as she'd imagined. Somehow, the letters from the *Bruderrath* gave her the impression the town was a mini-metropolis. While Baltimore was no Washington City or New York, this was indeed no comparison to even the meanest of towns. A hamlet, to be sure, but not much more.

Still, the train depot was a blessing, right here in the middle of—er, the village.

The train stopped amid a screeching of wheels on iron rails and a cloud of smoke. When she finally saw her surroundings outside the windows again, the fresh coat of paint on the station cheered her.

Perhaps the remainder of the town would look as well-maintained.

She stood and hefted her case in one hand, her reticule hanging from her other wrist by its drawstring. Glad she'd chosen not to pack the bag with much more than her textbook and a few personal necessities, she waited her turn to step down into her new life. Three other passengers alighted from her car, and she stepped onto the platform. Brand assisted her to a bench outside the depot building, and she sat, uncertain what to do next.

She'd exchanged three letters with the governing board. The final enclosed her train ticket and the offhand mention that somebody would meet her. No name. No description.

She studied each person moving about the area, offering them what she hoped was a sincere smile. However, as the minutes ticked past and the numbers of individuals conducting business diminished, so did her hopes of being greeted by a friendly face.

Then the train pulled out, and Brand waved to her.

She would miss him.

The sweltering sun beat down on her, and rivulets of sweat ran down her spine. Her tongue stuck to the roof of her mouth, whether from fear or thirst she wasn't certain. A horse and wagon neared, and with it, her hopes rose. Perhaps this was—

But no. The driver nodded in her direction but continued in the direction of the town.

She pulled the letters from her reticule and extracted the most recent missive, scanning it for details she'd missed in prior readings. Well, she had the correct date and location. September the seventh. Homestead, Iowa.

What else?

Apparently the elders were neither verbose nor effusive, since the wording was spare and any excitement they might have shared at her arrival was carefully disguised.

Nothing.

Checking to make certain nobody loitered nearby who might choose this moment to steal her suitcase, she gripped her travel bag and purse and headed inside the building.

She paused as she crossed the portal to allow her eyes to adjust to the dim interior. To her left, a counter now marked CLOSED. Three benches lined the walls. An unlit stove sat in the middle of the room, connected to the outside by a black pipe leading toward the roof. Bare rafters overhead. A scarred wooden floor. A spittoon in one corner. An abandoned newspaper on a windowsill. A door leading to the baggage room, another to the lavatory, and a third marked OFFICE.

"Hello. Is anybody here?"

Her voice echoed in the compact space. She took another few steps in the direction of the first doorway. Perhaps the stationmaster was in there, sorting parcels and mail bags. She pushed open the door, whose hinges screamed like a banshee.

"Anybody in there?"

When she received no answer, she turned toward the office, knocked, and opened that door. Outfitted with furniture, but nobody there, either.

She was alone. In a tiny town in the middle of nowhere.

Tears threatened to overflow, and she dabbed with her lace handkerchief at her eyes and nose. If her contact appeared now, he'd find a woman with blotchy cheeks and bloodshot eyes. And he'd likely put her on the next train east. How humiliating—losing her job before she even started.

* * *

Seth Seibel gritted his teeth as he pushed the *Rollstuhl* up the slight incline to the train depot. A fine time for the *Bruderrath* to advise him he needed to meet the town's new nurse. Five minutes before her arrival. This was no way to impress this young woman. Which they sorely needed to do if she was to be convinced to stay. Unlike the last three nurses who came and stayed less than three months each. Not that they needed a nurse. No, God would heal those He chose to heal, and the rest would experience their permanent healing in heaven.

He dipped his head to study the crown of his son's. Hair the color of golden prairie wheat. Just like his *mutter.* Skin pale and freckled. Like hers. Eyes as green as grass in May. The only part of him in his son.

He pressed on. The elders said healing here or healing there mattered little to a divine God Who was always right in His decisions and actions.

So why did the thought of losing his son fill him with such dread?

And why did he waffle when it came to choosing faith or hoping in medicine for healing? Did his failure to

14

take a stand mean his faith wasn't strong enough? And if that were true, the salvation of his eternal soul stood in jeopardy.

Surely a loving God wouldn't provide medicine and doctors—and now even a nurse—to entrap His children?

He sighed. He had no answers. He had no choice. This was his life, and he must endure it as best he could. Heaven knew his turmoil.

Life in the Amana Colonies wasn't easy for those born here and surely was even more difficult for an outsider. There were those Amanites who didn't welcome those not of their faith. And although commanded to love all people—well, he found it troublesome to follow that Biblical law himself at times. Even his own people sometimes were—er, prickly.

Caleb turned in his seat and grinned up at him. "Papa, will we be there soon?"

"Yes. Just a little while."

The nine-year-old, with the body of a boy two years younger and the heart of a saint, faced forward, gripping the arms of the chair as it bounced over rocks and into ruts. Normally Seth wouldn't subject his child to this torture, but today he had no choice. The immediacy of his mission left no time to arrange for care for his invalid son.

Then Seth's beseeching pleas to be allowed to accompany him overrode any argument he might have concocted. The boy was home from *Kindershule* today because of a slight fever this morning. Already invalided to this chair and behind in his studies because of his severe asthma—the same disease that claimed the child's mother and Seth's beloved wife Anna—Seth had little hope the child would advance with his peers this year. Perhaps a few days of rest at home would do Caleb good. And him, too, as he was relieved from most of his regular duties to tend to his son. If Anna were here—well, many things would be different if that were the case.

Another rock, and Caleb gasped. "Papa, slow down. We're not in a race."

Sweat dribbled down Seth's forehead, burning his eyes. He paused, removed his hat, and swabbed at his face with his handkerchief, already damp and not even noon. "Okay, now we press on again." He tapped Caleb's shoulder. "And yes, we are late. Nurse Mayer will already be waiting for us."

His son gripped imaginary reins and slapped them against his invisible horse's rump. "Giddy-up, horse. Go faster."

Seth grinned. Despite his pale skin and lack of strength or breath, his son's sharp mind still astounded him.

Must have gotten that from his mutter.

They rounded the last bend in the road leading to the train depot and slowed. Not a living soul in sight. Not even a stray dog. Had he gotten the time wrong? Perhaps the *Bruderrath* mistook the date?

Well, now that they were here, he'd stop at the

lavatory to rinse his kerchief and get them both a drink of water.

He aimed the wheeled chair toward the door into the station. "We'll rest in here a moment. If she isn't here, another will return for her later."

Caleb turned, his cheeks pink from the sun and heat. "You said she was coming today, Papa. You said she would make me well." He pointed. "There's a trunk. Do you think it's hers?"

"Maybe. Or perhaps it arrived for another resident." He patted the boy's shoulder. "And yes, I said that. But maybe I was wrong." He clutched the back of the chair and tipped it back. "Hold on. Over the bump."

The wheels thunk-thunked over the threshold and into the open room. The ticket station and the office were both empty, so he headed for the lavatory and the cool water in the jug and basin there.

Perhaps the nurse had second thoughts and decided not to come. The town was probably better off without her. Let them put their trust in God for their healing.

Right. Like he'd done.

He paused at a rustle in the corner and peered through the gloom.

A woman, huddled on the bench, chin tucked to her chest. Past middle age. Her dress wrinkled. Sniffling.

He stepped closer, pushing the chair ahead of him. Surely this wasn't the nursing professional they'd hired to heal the sick. To make his son well. One strong and

17

courageous enough to travel from the east coast to their colonies would also bravely wait a few minutes. He glanced at the clock over the front door. Very well, an hour.

In the heat. In a town strange to her.

"Are you Nurse Mayer?"

Please say you're not. Please be somebody's maiden aunt who alighted at the wrong station and awaits the next scheduled train. Or please be waiting for somebody other than me.

Perhaps if he was a little rude, she'd decide this wasn't the town for her. If she left before anybody befriended her, it would be better for everybody. Better Caleb not become attached to another woman who would leave him.

Better for him not to get his hopes up that anything except a miracle from God could save his son.

Her head raised, and she shoved her handkerchief into a sleeve before standing. "Yes, I am." She crossed the distance between them in three quick steps. "I was so worried I'd gotten the wrong town or—"

He chuckled. "Or the wrong date. Exactly what I thought as I came." He stepped aside at a tugging on his pants leg. "This is my son, Caleb."

She squatted down, the skirt of her dress flounced around her like the finest ball gown. Up close, she wasn't so old as he'd first thought, and the smile she bestowed on the child melted away his misgivings.

If he'd had any doubts before, the rapturous expression on Caleb's face washed them all away.

His son had just fallen in love with the new nurse. Who was he to send her away?

Chapter 2

Despite the rough start to her new life in this town, Tessa loved the boy immediately. His quick smile and love of life were infectious. Although his father seemed immune. Standing by, hands shoved in his pockets. Not smiling at the boy's antics and jokes.

What kind of father was he?

Or perhaps this was the type she'd expect in a closed religious community. She was no stranger to the concept—having been raised in a Mennonite environment—yet the man's stoicism was obvious. Another reason for choosing this assignment—she spoke some German, the mother tongue of many of the older residents.

After a few minutes, in which she gave Caleb permission to address her as Nurse Tessa, she straightened. "Thank you for coming to fetch me."

"I was told to come."

And what exactly did that mean? That he had no choice? Was forced to meet her out of compulsion, rather than choice?

Miss Harrow's words of advice returned to her memory: No matter the greeting, from patient or family, smile. None can argue with a smile.

Tessa pasted on a smile she didn't feel. Until she glanced at the son again. And then she couldn't hold back. Her cheeks hurt with the grin that surely needed releasing after the day she'd had.

Caleb held a hand to her. "Come on, Nurse Tessa. We're taking you to your permit house."

She gripped the boy's hand. His skin, at once dry and feverish, then cold and clammy, told her far more than did the child when she'd asked him how he felt today. His quick claim of feeling finer than peach fuzz wasn't quite true. The journey from their home in one of the villages to the train station had exhausted him. Perhaps she'd find them something to eat and drink in the residence she'd call home while here.

When they reached the door, she relinquished her hold and stepped outside, then stopped short. Her trunk. Without a wagon, they couldn't carry it between them. And she wouldn't leave it. No telling what might happen to it. In Baltimore, it would have sprouted legs by now and disappeared.

She turned to Mr. Seibel. "My trunk."

Caleb patted his legs. "Put it here."

She shook her head. "Oh, no, I don't think—"

But the boy persisted. "We do it all the time, don't we, Papa?" He ran his hands along the chair's arms. "See, it will balance here. It won't even touch my legs."

Tessa saw he was correct. His limbs were so thin from lack of use that there was no danger of his being crushed by the case. "Very well. If your father can help me, I think we can get it there."

Mr. Seibel nodded. "It's a downhill ride into town, Caleb, so it should be quicker than coming here."

"It's okay, Papa. I'm not tired."

Now Tessa knew he didn't speak the whole truth. The dark circles under his eyes, heavy lids, slumped shoulders, and bluish lips and fingernail beds all shouted exhaustion.

She ruffled the boy's hair. "But I am. So let's get me home, and perhaps we'll find a cool drink and a cookie or two. How does that sound?"

The youngster straightened and grinned. "Finer than—"

"Peach fuzz." Tessa joined in his favorite saying. "Mr. Seibel?"

The man finally allowed his mouth to turn up at the corners. He was really not so stern looking when his face relaxed. About her own age, perhaps a year or so older. His work-roughened hands bespoke a strong ethic of supporting his family and earning a living. And his son obviously adored him. His wife was a lucky woman.

23

A lump in her throat threatened to cut off her breathing, and she turned to address the trunk. "If I grab this handle, perhaps you—"

Instead, Mr. Seibel squatted and grabbed the handles, straightened his legs, and turned, all in one quick motion. And before she said a word, the trunk rested on the chair, exactly as Caleb prophesied. Then the man gripped the back of his son's wheeled chair and pushed, straining with the additional weight, heading toward town.

At a spot in the road when a wheel went down in a rut, the trunk tilted. Bracing her shoulder to its side, she maintained its position until they straightened out and continued on their way again.

She pumped her arms like a strong man at a circus. "Good thing I am strong."

Mr. Seibel said nothing, but his snort spoke volumes.

She planted her hands on her hips and glared at him, making sure to include a half-smile to soften her words. "Well, I am."

Caleb nodded and mimicked her muscle man impersonation. "Me, too. See my muscles."

His words stung because, in fact, he had little body mass at all. Still, he believed he did, and in her experience, faith was often the difference between a dream and a disaster.

She tapped his bicep. "You are strong as an ox. Just like your papa."

The words slipped out, and instantly she wished she could snatch them back. What must he think of a single woman making such inappropriate comments about a married man she'd just met?

She groaned, and heat raced up her cheeks as she dropped her gaze. When he didn't respond, she risked a glance from the corner of her eye.

How infuriating. He was smiling. No, not smiling. Grinning. Biting his lip as though buttoning in an outright guffaw.

Was her humiliation the only thing that would draw a positive response from him?

Well, he'd best enjoy this moment, because from now on, she'd keep a tight rein on her tongue.

If he was counting on her slip-ups to find reason to laugh, this would be the last of his jocularity for a long time.

* * *

Seth knew better than to laugh out loud. From what he knew about women—which would fill a thimble maybe twice—they didn't appreciate being the brunt of a joke.

And if he wanted this one to stay—at least until his son was well—then he'd best watch himself.

Still, her reaction to her unregulated response was interesting. And refreshing. In the colonies, interaction between unrelated men and women was few and far between. Frowned on, in fact, unless the couple was courting. Even that was closely monitored to ensure nothing untoward happened.

Who was this woman that she was so sensitive to the ways of the colony? Perhaps Amish? Or Mennonite? Was she accustomed to their ways? Was that why she was here?

He shook his head as they slowed at the gate of the permit house assigned to Nurse Mayer. No, she was here in answer to Anna's prayers. And not hers only, of course. Many in the colonies had prayed for a nurse ever since their doctor died in the cholera epidemic two years ago. Someone to bandage a cut, stitch a gash, splint a break, and help an overworked midwife.

Not his prayers. No, God stopped listening to his inadequate pleas as Anna lay on her deathbed, succumbing to yet another asthmatic attack. He'd bargained with the Almighty, cajoled Him, threatened Him, offered money—all to no avail.

He had nothing the Creator wanted or needed—except, apparently, his wife. And now, perhaps, his son.

Day by day Caleb's health worsened. A little more out of breath. Skin more pale. Less interested in eating in the communal kitchen where they dined apart, men on one side, women and children on the other.

No, God didn't hear *him*.

Nurse Mayer opened the gate and led them up the walkway before opening the door and stepping inside. Seth lowered the trunk to the veranda—it was too wide to go in the way it was—then pushed his son's chair in before hauling the case inside.

The nurse busied herself in the kitchen. "Would you like hot tea? I also have milk and water, courtesy of the colonies."

He removed his hat. "Water is good. For both of us."

She gestured to him. "Come in. Plenty of room."

The permit house was similar to his own, with a stove and hearth, a table and chairs, a work table, and a small cabinet with two tin cups and a can of crackers. Unlike his, this house had no upper floor. In the far corner, the bed. Would she find the straw-filled mattress to her liking?

Heat ran up his neck at the sight of the sleeping arrangements out in the open. He shouldn't be thinking about the nurse and her bed.

She cleared her throat softly. "I don't see any food except these biscuits."

He nodded. "Each colony has several communal *küche*—kitchens. Today the *küchebaas*—" He struggled for the right words. Why hadn't he noticed how her eyes were so much like Anna's—and yet so different? Brown as the soil, yet tinged with gray. "Kitchen boss will visit to tell you the rules."

"Rules?" Her brow pulled down. "Will I have a schedule to cook?"

He chuckled. "No. You are a guest, first of all. And second, you are a nurse. Far too busy to cook. But you will eat in one of the kitchens. Three meals a day, and two snacks, if you choose."

"Are there other rules I need?"

How much should he say? Perhaps it would be best if he left that to others. Her piercing gaze and soft skin were too distracting.

"The elders will tell you what you need to know." He turned to his son. "Drink your water, then we must return home. I have work to do before dinner."

She followed them to the door. "Will I see you in the kitchen?"

"No. We live in High Amana. We have our own kitchens there. Each colony is independent, so we rarely go to others unless we're visiting."

Her smile dropped. "Oh." She scanned the street. "Where is my office?"

"Your office?"

"Where I will see patients."

"In their homes, of course. They are sick and will be at home. Few will visit you here."

Her eyebrows shot up, disappearing beneath the bonnet covering her hair that threatened to loose its bonds. "Oh."

Caleb tugged on his pants leg again. "Papa, maybe we can visit tomorrow if I'm still feeling poorly." He looked up at the nurse. "Will that be all right, Nurse Tessa?"

She bent until she met him straight on. "If you are

still unwell, I will come visit you. See your house. Meet your mother."

Seth's heart thudded to the toes of his boots. She didn't know. Well, of course not. How could she? Unlikely the *Bruderrath* would write her a detailed history of each family.

He shuffled his feet, his eyes on his son. How would Caleb handle this breach of their privacy? Once a person passed in the colonies, their name was rarely spoken. He wasn't certain where this custom originated, but that didn't stop him from thinking about Anna almost every minute of every day. Wondering what her reaction would have been in a particular situation. Hoping she was pleased with how their son was growing up. Keeping an eye on him as he struggled some days to stay positive for Caleb.

His son stared at her for a moment then sighed. "Do you know my *mutter*?"

"No, Caleb. But to have such a wonderful boy as you, she must be very special."

Caleb smiled. "She is. She's in heaven now, waiting for me." He struggled to draw a deep breath but failed, then slumped in his chair. "Sometimes I don't think she'll have to wait a long time." He crooked a finger, beckoning her to draw near. "But don't tell my papa. I wouldn't want to leave him alone."

She placed a forefinger across her lips. "I won't say a word."

The boy's words acted like additional nails in Seth's

heart. He was the adult. The one who should worry about his child.

Not the other way around.

Chapter 3

Tessa followed the instructions from Mary, the Küchebaas for her permit house, and arrived at the dining hall before the last gong of the bell for supper died away. She nodded to those who acknowledged her, but remained silent. Mary said mealtimes were for eating, and not for dithering, as she put it.

The kindly older woman also dropped a few hints for what to expect in the hall. Potatoes, cold chicken, and *Katerbohnen*—yellow dill bean salad with eggs and sour cream dressing—were on Monday evening's menu. Each day of the week had its own pre-set food which changed according to the season and availability. The colonies worked hard to remain self-sufficient, bringing in only those foods and goods they didn't produce themselves.

She slipped into an empty spot on the end of the bench in the women and children's section of the room. About a dozen women and the same number of children occupied the other seats, while on the far side of the area sat twenty or so men.

Tessa smiled at the woman to her left, but when no introduction was made, she remained silent. No doubt word had already spread that the new nurse was in town. She caught the eye of a boy about Caleb's age on the opposite side. The child peeked out from around his mother's arm, and when she smiled and waggled her eyebrows at him, he ducked back out of sight.

She sighed, hoping she would soon not be an object of curiosity, but instead a vital component to the health and well-being of all the colonies.

After prayers were spoken over the meal—in German—she accepted and passed bowls of food along. Although raised in the Mennonite tradition, her father insisted they speak English, but she knew a few words. Still, from what she remembered, the prayer was one of thanksgiving and gratitude for the food and for their individual sanctification.

She bent her head to the task of eating while keeping one eye on the others around her. She surely didn't want to do anything to offend someone, or break a rule, or commit a taboo. Not on her first day. Not ever, for that matter.

The other women wore bonnets that covered the backs of their heads, and long-sleeved blouses with high necks. Older girls dressed similarly, while the children wore outfits that mimicked their parents'—girls in dresses with no frills or ribbons, boys in a white shirt and dungarees. Practical, sturdy, modest, easy to sew at home. Even buttons were plain. Not a sparkle or a bright bit in sight.

She slid her empty plate to her left and accepted a cup of something hot from the woman across from her. A plate of cookies made its way down the length of the table, a sight that made the children squirm in anticipation. Mothers hushed their broods, casting a glance in her direction. She offered them what she hoped was a smile that assured them she wasn't discomfited by the youngsters' action. However, more than once a disapproving glare was their response.

And then, from the far end of the table, came a small voice. "Nurse Tessa. I'm here."

She turned in the direction where a hand waved. "Caleb."

A wave of gasps echoed through the room, which then fell silent. A man cleared his throat at a table behind her—Mr. Seibel? Or one of the elders? Her greeting died in her throat. Would they evict her from the balance of the meal? From dining with them forever?

Had she just made her first critical error?

And what was he doing here? Surely he and his father didn't travel the several miles just to eat in Homestead?

The woman sitting next to Caleb hushed him with a sharp, whispered admonition. "Be quiet or you'll be punished."

33

Caleb's attendant waited until almost everybody else left before standing and pushing his chair toward the door. Tessa followed her out amid a barrage of questions from Caleb.

"Nurse Tessa, did you like the food? Monday's are my favorite day because I like *Katerbohnen*. Do you like bean salad?" He twisted and turned in his chair to keep her in sight. "Papa is waiting over there for us. Can you come visit us tonight? I hope you like books. I'm learning, and Papa says I'm a good reader. Can I read for you?" He gestured to the woman who sat with him at supper. "Melody doesn't like reading, do you, Melody?"

The young woman peered at the boy, a smirk marring her otherwise-perfect countenance. "I like what you like, Caleb."

For some reason, however, her pronouncement didn't bring a smile to the boy's face.

Finally they cleared the building and stood to one side so they didn't slow others anxious to return home.

Tessa scooted down beside the boy. "You must have had a good rest when you got home today." She stood when Mr. Seibel joined them. "I didn't expect to see you here. I thought you live in High Amana?"

He glanced at the woman accompanying Caleb, who ducked her chin and smiled. "We do. But we can visit other colonies as we choose." He looked around. "One of the other farmers has a bull I might rent for stud on my cows." Red blotches dotted his neck and raced toward his ears at the mention of his purpose. "I mean—and Caleb wanted to visit his friends, too."

Tessa bit back a chuckle and struggled to not smile at the man's reaction to his own words. While stud fees wasn't a general topic of conversation in Baltimore, she was a nurse, after all, and knew how these things worked. "It's good to see you again, Mr. Seibel."

"Please, call me Seth."

She wasn't certain how easily she could make that transition. Calling him Mister helped keep their relationship on a more formal footing. Held him at arm's length.

Because two things were abundantly clear: She adored his son. And her feelings for the father were growing. She liked being around him.

Calling him by his Christian name might make her look for reasons to seek him out.

And look where that had gotten her in the past.

Here, with a broken heart.

* * *

What was he thinking? Talking about animal husbandry with this beautiful and educated woman. She must think him an inconsiderate oaf. Or a country bumpkin. Or an idiot.

Or all three.

Melody sidled to stand at his side, and he resisted the urge to put more space between them. The last time he did that, she gripped his hand and dug in her fingernails as though tattooing her ownership upon him.

But she didn't own him. And although she was one of nicer eligible young women in the colonies, there was something about her he couldn't put his finger on. Unable to identify precisely what was off-putting about her, he used any excuse to keep his distance.

She seemed intent on not giving up and introduced herself to Nurse Mayer. "I'm Melody Leeken. *Very* good friend of Seth and Caleb." She bent, her face close to his son's, and smiled. "Aren't I, Caleb?"

The boy drew back as if he smelled something unpleasant. Perhaps that was what put Seth off the woman—the way his son withdrew from her. Still, her company was preferable to his son eating alone or unsupervised, and was but a short-term compromise. Once Caleb reached his thirteenth birthday, he would join his father at the men's tables.

Seth studied Nurse Mayer for her reaction. Surely such a discerning woman would detect anything untoward about Melody? And was that—yes. Her glance from his son to him and back to Caleb. He peered at her, but she pasted on a smile.

"Nice to meet you, Melody. Thank you for taking such wonderful care of Caleb."

The woman had the audacity to wave off the nurse's words like a pesky fly. "Oh, I'd do anything for Seth."

Had she really stressed the *any*? Perhaps he needed to find another woman to sit with his son. One of the married ones, maybe. An older widow. Then again, at nine, the boy could manage on his own once he set him at the table.

"So, Nurse Mayer." His words caught in his throat. How he wished he could address her by her first name. But she'd granted that privilege only to Caleb. No, he'd best keep his distance. At least in social situations. "Do you have your first patients lined up?"

"I'm meeting with the elders in a few minutes, and I expect they'll tell me my schedule. I feel at loose ends. I'm accustomed to a hospital or clinical setting."

Melody pressed her shoulder against his arm in an alarmingly intimate way. "I could never be a nurse. I don't like the sight of blood." She giggled. "That's why they put me in that stinky old laundry."

Seth sighed. The truth was the girl was bone-lazy. She'd already been assigned to several positions, including in the field, in the weaving shop, and now in her current assignment. She never lasted more than a few days. Which was strange, since she came from a family of twelve. As the third child, perhaps she'd found a way to shirk her duties at home without her parents knowing. He'd heard rumors, but tried to stay away from gossip. Difficult in a closed community, to be sure.

He tried again. "If the elders agree, perhaps I'll bring Caleb around tomorrow."

Melody's bottom lip jutted out. "But I thought you would help me with firewood tomorrow."

His brow pulled down. "Tuesday isn't laundry day."

She shrugged and gave him a half-smile. "There was so much washing today we couldn't get it all done."

He noted her use of the term *we*, as if every woman in the laundry was to blame. Unlikely. He knew them. They were hard-working and committed to their job. No, more likely, *she* hadn't completed her task. Mostly because she didn't like the work assigned to the laundry the other days of the week, including pressing the linens, sewing repairs, and working in the kitchen gardens.

Nurse Mayer clasped her hands together. "I would love to see you—" She caught his eye, smiled down at Caleb, then included Melody in the invitation. "Whenever you are free. You know where to find me."

Melody looped her arm through his. "Yes, we do. Thank you."

She squeezed his bicep between her fingers, not so hard that he'd yelp, but enough to leave a bruise. That nobody would see beneath his long-sleeved shirt.

He pried her fingers loose. "Come, Caleb. You have school work to catch up with."

Melody placed her hand on top of his where it rested on the back of his son's chair. "I'll help. I'm very good at my letters."

"We don't want to take you from your own home duties, do we, Son?"

Caleb shook his head. "Can Nurse Tessa come and hear me read?"

Tessa kneeled beside the boy and patted his hand. "Perhaps. But I might be late. I must go talk to the elders now."

His eyes widened. "You're not in trouble because I called out to you, are you?"

She laughed. "No, this meeting was arranged before that happened."

"Okay then." Caleb turned to look up at him. "Let's go home, Papa." He glanced at Melody then back to him. "It's just we men tonight."

Melody harrumphed and stomped her foot. "Fine. I know when I'm not wanted."

Oh, no. The last thing he needed was for this disgruntled female to spread around the colonies that he—or Nurse Mayer—had been rude to her. When, in fact, she was the one who'd infiltrated herself into his plans.

As much as he disliked himself at this moment, he must make amends. "Let's sit by the river for a bit, shall we?"

The nurse headed toward the meeting hall and they turned in the opposite direction. If he had his way, the two women would change places.

And maybe—just maybe—it would be Melody who would be chastised by the elders while he stole a few minutes alone with his son's new best friend.

Just to get to know her better.

For Caleb's sake.

So why did guilt create an ache in his chest at the

39

thought of seeking another woman's company? As though he were unfaithful to Anna.

And why didn't he feel the same way about Melody? Likely because he felt nothing for that spoiled child.

But Nurse Mayer—she was completely different.

* * *

Tessa descended the steps from the meeting hall and turned toward home. Well, that wasn't so bad. Either word hadn't reached the *Bruderrath* about her *faux pas* at the evening meal, or they chose to overlook it. Perhaps for this one time only. She'd be more careful from now on.

Truth was, after the excitement about graduating from nursing school, the long days of travel, the strain of not being met at the station, then settling in at her house and the communal dining, she was worn to a frazzle.

And then this hour-long meeting with nine bearded men who governed Homestead. Her head fairly spun. Surely they'd verbally explained at least a hundred rules, including three she'd already broken: bonnet to be worn at every meal and at church meetings. No speaking during meals. No fraternizing with men.

And ninety-seven more. She should have taken notes.

She glanced at the single sheet of paper they'd given her, covered on both sides with—she checked the bottom of the second side—forty two of the most important rules. Some of which didn't even apply to her. Such as staying home for two years with her newborn—which she didn't even have—before returning to her assigned task half days until the child entered school, at which time she'd resume full-time work. With no husband in mind or even in sight, that would be one rule easy to obey.

She giggled at the thought of some of the others, particularly aimed at the men and boys. Suspenders instead of a belt. Shirt on at all times, no matter how high the temperatures. She was glad to be a woman.

The road led her over a bridge, and she slowed to admire the vista before her. Alone with her thoughts. In her new home. She stared into the sky. Tiny pinpricks of light reminded her that the same stars she gazed at in Baltimore now hovered overhead. Each one created by God. Named by Him. As were each and every one of His children.

Like Mr.—Seth. And Caleb. Even Melody. Seth, so polite and such a peacemaker. Caleb, whose imagination and love of life far exceeded his physical capabilities.

She sighed. And Melody. Obviously mean-spirited, the girl had set her cap for Seth. But why? He would be at least ten years older. Already encumbered with another woman's child. She could have the pick of anybody in the villages. One of the elders at the meeting tonight seemed more suited to her in terms of age.

But perhaps she liked a man who was more tender and less rigid. An elder would not only be tasked with keeping his wife and children in line, but must be seen to accomplish that task, as well. Another rule she'd learned tonight.

As a single woman without family, she was accountable to and under the rule and instruction of the *Bruderrath*, which both frightened and intimidated her. Nine men telling her what she could and couldn't do—heavens!

She turned to continue her trek but stopped when a woman's voice drifted up from the riverbank below.

Melody.

"But Seth, we were meant for each other. I mean, I have so much to offer a man."

Coming from anybody else, that might have been taken for a compliment to the man. But from her, an underlying insinuation muddied its meaning. Dirtied her statement.

"I'm not ready to consider courting, yet. My wife has only been gone—"

"Two years. You probably also remember exactly how many months and days. Well, she's dead, Seth. Dead."

"Keep your voice down. Caleb doesn't need to hear our conversation."

"Well, maybe I should just go over there and ask him if he'd like a new *mutter*. I bet he's tired of not having a soft shoulder to cry on. He'd like a gentle hand to comb his hair or clean the dirt from his skinned knee."

Seth chuckled. "He wouldn't skin his knees. He can't walk more than a few feet."

"Well, maybe he'd like to have a little brother or

sister."

Seth gasped. "Melody, that is not a suitable topic between us. We are not courting. We should not talk about such things."

"Surely you think about it. After all, you were married. And I'm sure you enjoyed all the advantages. If you know what I mean."

A snort of disgust was his only response to her. His voice faded, then the crunch of the wheeled chair on the walkway neared. They were coming this way. Tessa turned and trotted toward her house. How embarrassing if they discovered her eavesdropping. Not that such a thing was her intention. No, she stopped only to look at the stars.

She slowed when she figured she was out of earshot, then glanced behind her. Seth and Melody walked side by side, Melody's arm once again looped through his. The girl tipped her head at something he said, then he laughed with her.

Not much of a lover's spat, then, so quickly made up.

If only all of life's problems were so easily solved

Chapter 4

Tuesday morning, Tessa rose early and ate in the communal dining room. She scanned the area, hoping to catch a glimpse of Seth and Caleb, but they weren't present. She chided herself for looking for the pair. Hadn't Seth—Mr. Seibel seemed much more appropriate, particularly as it seemed his son would be a patient—made a point of explaining his presence? He'd come to visit somebody else. A farmer friend. With a bull.

She forced down the fried potatoes along with coffee and a delicious whole grain bread. Too bad her appetite didn't quite match the generous portions. She glared at the remaining golden, greasy medallions on her plate. At this rate, she'd be here until next meal.

She looked up and checked out the other women and children dining at the table with her. As she'd done yesterday, Melody sat at the far end. Did she live in Homestead, too? Or had she come from another colony hoping to see Seth—Mr. Seibel—today as well?

The younger woman caught her glance and offered an insincere smile—almost a smirk, really. Tessa swallowed a mouthful of breakfast and dropped her gaze. Yes, surely Caleb's father also graced their dining room yesterday to spend time with Melody. She was wholesome, pretty, and of a marriageable age. And she could be pleasant when she chose.

Still, there was something. . . Tessa shook off her ungracious thoughts. Just because he liked the woman didn't mean she shouldn't. They weren't competing with each other.

There, the final forkful. She pushed it down with the last of her coffee before passing the used utensils and dishes to her left. She covered her mouth to smother a tiny burp—what would her mother say about that?—and hurried outside. A quick trip home to change into her nursing uniform, then she'd begin her rounds.

Ten minutes later, donned in the white starched pinafore, navy cape, and white cap, the familiar mainstays of her profession, she headed toward Mrs. Agnes Walter, her first patient. Josiah Toms, an elder, gave her a list the previous day of those to visit first. The last nurse, having left some three weeks before, failed to provide comprehensive notes on those patients she'd medicine, so Tessa would rely on the patients themselves for their history and complaints.

When she knocked on Mrs. Walter's door, a frail

voice called for her to come in, which she did. Following the woman's instructions, she found her in a second-floor bedroom, propped up in bed, eating her breakfast.

Based on what was on the tray, somebody had delivered a meal similar to the one she'd consumed herself. However, in Mrs. Walter's case, she was consuming it with gusto.

Tessa set her nursing bag on the floor and settled into a chair beside the bed. "Good morning, Mrs. Walter. I'm Nurse Tessa."

She pronounced the woman's surname with a V instead of a W, as was common in the *Deutsche* language.

The elderly woman peered at her over the top of her cup. "I'm old and blind, young woman. Not deaf. You don't need to shout."

Sweat broke out on Tessa's upper lip, and she resisted the urge to swipe it away. Instead, she tied her hands into knots. Her second day here, and already she'd managed another *faux pas*. "Sorry. Please forgive me."

The old woman chuckled. "For that? No fears, child." She set her tray to one side, feeling for the edge of the bed first. "How are you today?"

"It's I who should be asking you that question, Mrs. Walter." She smiled. "But thank you for asking. I am well."

"Please, it's *Mutter* Agnes. That's what everybody calls me. And superb job of pronouncing my last name properly." She sniffed and looked out the window. "Most outsiders don't." She peered at her. "You're not one of us,

47

are you?"

Tessa chuckled. She suspected by the end of her appointment today, Mother Agnes would know more about the new nurse than said nurse knew about her patient. "I am not from the colonies, no. But I grew up Mennonite."

"That explains the accent. Close Old Order second cousins, as it were." Agnes settled against her pillow. "So you'll want to know all about me, I suppose?"

Tessa withdrew her notebook from her bag. She'd stayed up late the previous night dividing it into sections based on surname, so now she flipped almost to the end. "Yes. I apologize for my predecessors who didn't keep accurate records. Or if they did, they took them when they left."

"I don't think they wrote anything down. We've only had three nurses before you, and none lasted long. Barely long enough to learn their way around. So let's see. What do you really need?"

"Let's start with why they visited and what they did."

Over the next ten minutes of so, Mrs. Walter regaled Tessa with wildly improbable stories of late night visits, misdiagnoses, and nurses caught in delicate situations that were too many and too varied to be believed. When she finished, Tessa was in tears from laughing so much.

She swiped at her cheeks. "*Mutter* Agnes, you have brightened my day."

Agnes patted her hand. "Then I've accomplished

48

what I set out to do." She gestured to her. "Sit here beside me. I'm not contagious."

Tessa did as the woman bid, noting the thin legs and tiny form beneath the quilt. "Do you make an appointment so you can encourage folk, or are you in need of medical care?"

Mutter Agnes closed her eyes. "What I need won't be found in a pill or a potion, Child. Cheering you up has been medicine enough for me. And for you, too, I suspect." She reached over and stroked her cheek. "While my eyes no longer see, my spirit has perfect vision. I see you are carrying a cartload of hurt, Child." She dropped her hand to her lap. "No, you don't need to talk about it today. Perhaps the next time you visit. Or when you're ready."

"Well, I'd best make a few notes and listen to your heart and lungs. Earn my keep." Tessa pulled her stethoscope from her bag. She listened, moving its location, then nodded. "You have the lungs and heart of a woman twenty years younger."

"*Gutt. Gutt.* Then I should have many more years to bring my brand of medicine to my people."

Tessa smiled, knowing the woman couldn't see her expression, but unable to hold it back. How good God was to bring her here first thing today. Particularly after such a distressing evening and breakfast.

Perhaps He still heard her prayers, such as the ones asking that she fit into this new community. That she find staunch friends. Maybe even experience the love and joy of

49

family once again.

As she bid goodbye and left for her next appointment, two faces flashed across her mind.

Seth and Caleb.

Into which category would they fit?

* * *

From his seat in his workshop, Seth looked up when footsteps raced toward him. A young boy—one of the Risdins, he thought, with a slip of paper clutched in one hand, skidded to a stop, sending up a cloud of dust.

After setting down the leather traces and the punch tool, Seth clapped the boy on the shoulder. "What is the rush?"

In reply, the lad held out the hand containing the paper.

Seth accepted the note. "Thank you. Maybe you would come to our home later for a glass of lemon-ginger drink?" He quirked his chin in the direction of Caleb, who sat in his chair beneath the shade of a cottonwood tree, repairing the woven basket used to gather eggs. "I'm sure Caleb would enjoy your company."

The boy bobbed his head. "I'll check with my *mutter*."

Seth turned back to the note as the child ran off. Few of Caleb's school friends ever visited their home. If this one did—well, he could but pray.

He scanned the words. A summons to the elders before midday meal. To discuss an urgent matter.

He cast his mind over the past day or so, certain that any shortcoming on his part would not be left longer than that. No, discipline was fair but as immediate as practicable. They would not leave a matter to fester. But he could not identify any incident.

He glanced at Caleb. Was it possible that the boy—? He doubted very much whether that was the case. After all, they were together most of the time. Melody hadn't mentioned anything happening at dinner last evening. And he'd heard nothing from the others. Surely somebody would have said something.

He exhaled and glanced at the sun. Nearing noon. Time to wash up and head for the communal kitchen. Everything took longer with his son in the *Rollstuhl*. He'd best go now.

He tucked the note into his pants pocket then headed for Caleb, calling as he went. "Time to get cleaned up for dinner."

Caleb acknowledged him with a nod then turned back to his task, his brow furrowed and tongue sticking out of the side of his mouth. How much he looked like his mother. She had the same mannerism.

Seth gripped the chair and pushed, heading across the yard to their house. Outside the back door, a jug of water, basin, soap, and towel awaited.

He tapped his son on the shoulder. "Do you need the privy first?"

"No, Papa. But I am hungry."

"You're always hungry, little man."

Caleb smiled at the term as he always did. "And someday I'll be a big man like you, right, Papa?"

"Bigger than me. Like Goliath."

Seth's heart ached that his words always sounded and felt hollow to him. Did Caleb detect any note of insincerity? He never expressed such thoughts. But truthfully, Seth had little hope that his son would live any longer than Anna had. Maybe not as long, since his asthma attacks seemed more severe and closer together than hers.

At the washstand, Caleb soaped then washed and rinsed his hands and arms up to his elbows. He even splashed a little water on his face, then dried off with the towel.

He tipped his head up to smile at his father. "Your turn, Papa."

Seth ruffled the boy's hair then set to work to clean up at least as well as his son had. Once done, he turned the chair toward their communal kitchen, nodding to neighbors they met along the way.

When they arrived, still a few minutes early, he squatted down to meet his son's eyes. "I'll leave you here. I have to go see the elders."

Caleb studied his face. "Did I do something wrong again, Papa?"

Seth stood. "Not at all. You may be growing into the size of Goliath, but you have the heart of David. Remember, God said King David was a man after His own heart?"

"I do. My teacher told us that story."

"Wait here for me. If Miss Melody comes, you may go in with her. Or another woman."

"Hurry, Papa. I'm hungry, remember?"

Seth smiled and headed toward the meeting hall where the elders awaited. Surely if this were truly a serious matter, they would have sent one of their own with the message? And the meeting would be more than a few minutes, as the note suggested?

He drew several breaths, shrugging out the kinks in the back of his neck. No, this had to be some minor request. Perhaps they needed him to take a wagon of goods to the train in Homestead. Or pick up another person, as he'd done with Nurse Mayer.

Thinking of her as he walked the hundred or so feet to the hall filled him with a lightness of heart he'd not experienced since Anna passed. Even Melody, with her flirtatious looks and tantalizing eyes didn't hold a candle to the nurse. True, he knew little of her, but one thing was certain: She had a big heart. A love for God.

And a Grand Canyon-sized hurt in her past.

Up the steps and into the cool interior of the hall he strode. Five men clustered in a circle of chairs, with a single seat vacant.

His.

He nodded to each in turn then sat, his hat in his hands, waiting for them to speak. It was not their way to do otherwise.

After a minute or so, Abram Eaker, a man just a few years older than himself but blessed with a healthy wife and seven rambunctious children, cleared his throat. "Brother Seibel, we called you here today to discuss an important matter."

Seth straightened in his seat, the wooden spindles digging into his shoulder bones. "I am your servant."

Brother Abram nodded. "We—that is, the elders—have been discussing your situation."

His situation?

"And we believe it is time you married again."

He blinked several times, letting the words sink in. Courting? Courting who? And why this rush for him to wed? Tobias Gutner was widowed seven years before the elders relaxed the remarriage rules in cases of death. Prior to that, nobody remarried, and, in fact, marriage was deemed a serious spiritual failing by many.

"We have seen you spending time with Melody Leeken. She seems to like your son. And she is of marriageable age. We believe her father would be conducive to granting you the privilege of asking for her hand."

How to answer such a summons? He had no interest in Melody as a wife. And the fact she took Caleb to meals surely didn't qualify her to be his mother. His mouth went dry, and he could form no intelligible reply.

However, the elders mistook his lack of response as

54

his approval of their suggestions, because smiles overtook their previously somber expressions, and each one nodded as though he'd actually replied in the affirmative.

Inside, he screamed *No, No, No!*

Brother Abram broke the silence. "Unless there is another you would choose?"

Once again, Nurse Mayer sprang to mind. But no. She was an outsider. Not of their faith. To choose her would mean expulsion from the colonies. And while that might be preferable to him than wedding Melody, the loss of the only life he knew might kill his son.

He would stay.

He would do what was being asked of him.

He would court Melody.

Seth nodded. "I will pray on the matter."

The elders stood, and Brother Abram clapped him on the back. "We understand Anna was your first love, but life must go on. Melody will make you a good wife. And a wonderful mother for your son, and, eventually, for your other children. She comes from a—a fruitful family. Perhaps the sickness that claims Caleb will die with Anna, and your new family will be—shall we say—more productive?"

Sounds like they're hoping Caleb will do as Anna did. Remove the blot from our colony.

Yet he couldn't speak this aloud. They might think he agreed with them.

Which he could not—and would not—do.

55

* * *

From outside the meeting hall window, standing in the shade chatting with two women, Tessa overheard the elder's words. Her heart dipped into her boots at the implication. That somehow Anna's asthma was a curse on the colony.

She should have remained in Homestead. Surely there were more patients to see there today. But no, she decided to check in on Caleb and meet two expectant mothers before they delivered. While respiratory therapy was her chosen specialty—and the reason for her assignment in Amana—she also loved bringing babies into the world.

She sidled away from the window and turned her back when footsteps indicated the men's departure from the hall. Perhaps she'd find another communal kitchen to eat her meal—

"Nurse Tessa. Over there, Papa. See, she said she'd come to see us."

She turned at her name, unable to ignore the child in the chair who had already captivated her heart. But she must be diligent not to get too attached to the boy or his father—that was Melody's place, not hers.

No, she'd be careful not to encourage him. "Hello, Caleb."

A smudge of dirt dotted the end of his nose, a spot he'd missed when washing up for meal. She shoved her hands into her pockets. Otherwise, she might be tempted

56

to wipe off the bit of dust.

He waved and laughed as his father pushed him over the uneven ground. "Faster, Papa. I want to talk with her before meal begins."

The pair arrived, both out of breath and sweating from the exertion, and she smiled. "Good day, Mr. Seibel."

"Seth, remember." His chide held no hint of reproof. He nodded to the other two women, who smiled, bobbed their heads, and moved off to join another group. "I didn't expect to see you again so soon."

She shifted her nursing bag from one hand to the other. "I came to check on Caleb." She smiled down at the boy. "After meal, I'll listen to how well your lungs are doing."

He grinned from ear to ear. "Do you have one of those stetha—stetha—thingies where you can hear my heart, too?"

"I do." She hefted her kit. "In this bag. And I have a special treat for patients who are extra good."

He bounced in his chair. "I'm good, aren't I, Papa?"

The child's innocent question, so close on the heels of the sideways insinuation from Brother Abram, cut to Tessa's core. "Yes, you are very, very good."

The Küchebaas rang the handbell, summoning them to meal, and Tessa walked alongside the pair.

Before they reached the door, however, a lilting voice called out. "Seth, wait for me."

With those words, the sunshine of Tessa's day evaporated. She bid good-day to Caleb and his father and made her way to her usual spot at the end of the bench. Minutes later, Melody swished past, pushing Caleb's chair to their place at the opposite end. As far away from her as was possible and still be in the same room.

Surely not intentional? Although there were two seats closer, had the younger woman so chosen.

No, this was a better situation. Keep the man and his son at physical arm's length, as well as emotional. He had his marching orders, and she certainly wasn't here to upset the apple cart. Melody would make a good wife—the elders and the other wives would see to that—and there was no room for her in their lives.

Not now, while Seth and Melody commenced the courting stage of their relationship.

And perhaps never.

* * *

Later that afternoon, Seth worked in the potato field, harrowing between the rows to till the weeds under the soil. The sun beat down on him, and he paused several times to swipe his face and neck with his already-damp kerchief. His tongue stuck to the roof of his mouth, but the cause wasn't only the heat.

Ever since his meeting with the elders, he'd struggled to work out what he might say to Melody's father. His next step would be to ask the man's permission to court his oldest daughter. Without that, he should not broach the subject with her. Not that he had any doubts as to her answer. She'd made her wishes abundantly clear last evening down by the river.

Heat unrelated to the weather rose to his cheeks, and he swabbed again at them, wishing for a shade tree and a cool drink of sarsaparilla tea. Of all the marriageable women in the colonies, why had Melody come to their attention? Perhaps her father planted the idea? Or Melody herself? He wouldn't put it past her to feather her own cap by intimating he was interested but too bashful to speak up.

The horse-drawn machine bound up against something beneath the soil, and the draft animal stopped. Yet another delay. At this rate, he'd never finish. Or perhaps his mind was so preoccupied that he couldn't focus on his part in this operation.

He exhaled, muttering under his breath, before jumping to the ground and walking around the rear of the blades and tines. He assessed the situation and determined where the problem lay. Squatting down, he dug his fingers into the soil in front of a blade. Ah, yes. A rock. Sometimes he wondered if the rich Iowa soil grew more rocks than potatoes.

He scooped soil from the base of the obstruction and shoved his right hand into the hole, intent on removing the rock. If he could just grab a hold of the obstacle. . .

At that moment, the horse took it upon itself to shift position. The blade wedged his fingers against the rock.

He gritted his teeth against the pain and banged his other hand against the side of the wagon. "Whoa."

However, rather than doing as it was told, the beast chose to bolt.

Blades and tines raked across the back of his hand as the gear-engaged mechanism continued moving forward. A searing sensation, like hot coals, paralyzed his fingers. Unable to extract his hand, afraid to do so might sever his digits, Seth braced his shoulder against the wagon. Perhaps he could relieve the weight from its downward thrust.

In a moment, the machine passed him, and he collapsed on the ground. Recently turned soil, cool against his cheek, brought some relief. But his hand and arm were on fire.

Did he really want to see the damage? What if he'd lost a finger? Or a thumb? He'd be unable to work as before. And how long to heal? What would become of him and his son? Might the elders use this as the final evidence of a curse on his family and expel them from the community?

He opened one eye and peered at the sky. "God, if You can hear, please help me."

He closed his eye again and drew several deep breaths before pushing himself upright. His heart pounded in his ears, drowning out the birds gathered in the trees.

He looked around. Nobody within earshot to help. Well, then, he'd have to do it himself, since even God seemed to be elsewhere. Clenching his jaw, he flexed his fingers then grunted. Still excruciating, but at least they all seemed attached.

He pulled his hand from the hole. Blood poured from a dozen places. Bone exposed on his little finger, but didn't seem broken. Miraculously, his arm escaped unscathed, probably because of his long-sleeved shirt.

With his left hand, he yanked out his kerchief and wrapped it around his wounded hand. Staggering to his feet, he considered his next move. Dirt was ground deep into the wounds. The risk of infection was high. He needed cleaning. Stitching. Perhaps something for the pain.

Nurse Mayer was in High Amana this afternoon. Where did she say she was going after she'd checked out Caleb? To see Rebekka Eaker. Clutching his hand to his chest, he trotted in the direction of the woman's house. Hopefully, if she wasn't there, Sister Eaker would know where she'd gone.

Focusing on his destination and not the agony of his injury was all that bore him to the Eaker home. He collapsed on the front porch and used the last of his energy to call for help.

Nurse Mayer's face appeared as though hovering in the air like an angel. Perhaps he had died and gone to heaven. If so, Anna would be here. And his parents. And hers.

He opened his eyes. No, just Nurse Mayer and Sister Eaker.

Not heaven, then, for they lived and breathed.

But a refuge, for certain.

The nurse took immediate action. "Fetch my bag, please."

The very pregnant woman lumbered out of sight and returned with the leather kit bag, which she set on the porch.

Nurse Mayer withdrew a bottle and undid the cork stopper. "This will sting, but it will clean your wounds."

He nodded. Nothing could hurt as much as—he yelped. He was wrong. The cure stung more than the original injury. He bit his lip. His response had distressed her, judging by how her brow and mouth pulled down. He must be strong. Not detract her from her job.

She turned to Sister Eaker. "Will you boil water and bring clean rags?"

A quick nod and the woman returned inside.

Nurse Mayer unbuttoned his shirt cuff and examined his arm. "A few scratches but nothing a little soap and water won't fix." She smiled, her gaze serious. "Whatever did you do? You look like you took on a grizzly bear single-handedly."

"Harrowing machine."

"It's supposed to till the soil, not your hand."

"Oh, really? First day on the job for me."

His response brought an outright laugh which relieved the stress wrinkles around her eyes. And his.

Until she pulled a set of tweezers from her bag.

He groaned and turned his head away so he

couldn't see what she did next. By the time the sister returned with a basin of water and a handful of cloths, Nurse Mayer managed to touch every raw nerve ending and torn piece of flesh with the cold metal of her torture instrument.

But the effort was well worth it. Already his hand tingled less. Now an overall general ache infiltrated him from head to toe, a much-preferred sensation to the hot poker jabbing at him.

He caught the sister's eye. "Water, please."

She returned with a cup, and Nurse Mayer lifted his shoulders to enable him to drink. He downed the fluid thirstily. "More."

The nurse shook her head. "In a few minutes. Let that sit to make sure it won't come back up. Sometimes pain can make your stomach upset."

Her tone brooked no argument, and in any case, he had no energy to force the issue. He glanced at his hand. Swollen. Already bruising. Fingers like sausages. But now that the blood and dirt was cleared away, not looking too bad. "What was that devil spit you used?"

"Alcohol. It disinfects and cleans at the same time." She lowered her gaze and wrapped his hand in cloth. "Sorry."

"Did you learn about that in nursing school?"

"Yes. But I also learned from my mentor. A medical doctor. He subscribed to the ideas of Doctor Lister from France. That to fight infection, we must not wait for

63

the infection to take root, but instead we must treat the wound immediately."

"Infection is a normal part of healing, is it not?"

"No, it isn't. Normal healing involves the blood retaining access to the wound, to bring nutrients and oxygen, and to remove dead cells and waste products."

He turned his hand from left to right to survey it on all sides. "That makes sense."

She chuckled. "But modern medicine hasn't quite caught up with Dr. Lister. Some see his remedies as quackish."

"Perhaps they are, then."

She shook her head. "Not too many years ago, doctors bled patients, believing they were removing the waste and infection that way. We don't do that any longer because we realize that patients are usually left in a worse state. Leeches were once used, too, to suck out the bad."

"But we've progressed from those practices, haven't we?"

"Yes. But not until many doctors studied the effects of these treatments on their patients. Did you know that more men died on the operating table during the last war than were killed on the battlefield?"

He sat up. "I didn't."

She nodded this time. "Muskets and cannons wreak devastation on the human body. Most doctors saw no hope in any treatment other than amputation. Which, as you can imagine, is traumatic to an already-injured patient."

"But to attempt a treatment that's never been proven? Why, that could kill the person, too."

"If death is the only other option, it makes little difference. But the possibility of success in a more radical, if untried, procedure, should be enough to warrant an attempt."

Uncertain whether or not he agreed, he chose to remain neutral. Mostly because he didn't have the energy—or the medical knowledge she possessed—to argue. "Can you get me on my feet?"

"No, but I will assist you into a chair." She looped an arm under his shoulder and became a living crutch until he could get on his feet, whereupon she released him into a rocking chair nearby. "Good. If your stomach is stable, we'll get you another cup of water." While Sister Eaker fetched that, she peered into his eyes, lifted his eyelids, and moved her fingers back and forth for him to follow. "You appear in good condition. I recommend you rest here for an hour, sleep if you choose. I can fetch several men to convey you to your home."

He shook his head. "I have work to finish. A field to harrow."

She planted her hands on her hips. "Not today. Maybe tomorrow. If you rest."

Funny how her sternest expression was still gentle as a kitten's. He suspected she had neither fangs nor claws.

Not that he wanted to test her. At least, not right now.

He leaned his head back, weak as a newborn from getting up off the porch. Maybe she was right. He'd take a brief rest, then he'd sneak back to work.

In a few minutes.

Chapter 5

The next morning, Tessa raced down the road from Amana East, her nursing bag banging her leg with every step.

Oh, God, please. Let me get there in time.

Caleb, in the hayfield with his father, had collapsed. Choked on something, the lad said who fetched her from where she made her rounds with patients. Well, none of them were not breathing, so they could wait.

She slowed as she entered the town limits, scanning the fields on either side of the road as she trotted along, her breath coming in gasps. Unfamiliar with the names of the fields and locations, the boy's instruction of James Bauer's hay field meant little to her.

Goodness, she needed to get more exercise. The years of working alongside Dr. Betz, then studying in medical school until his death, hadn't prepared her to run the mile or two between colonies.

Or perhaps the actual problem was the ache behind

her ribs as she envisioned her small friend struggling to breathe. Afraid when he couldn't. Panicked he might never again.

She spotted the wagon filled with hay bales and veered off the main road. Several men stood in a huddle, while one kneeled beside a small form on the ground beneath a tree. At least they'd had the sense to place him in the shade.

Her mind played over the possibilities. Asthma attack, of course, was first on her list. That she could probably deal with. Insect sting. Snake bite. If either of those were the culprit, she had an uphill battle to fight. Actual choking—that she might be able to handle, too, having once performed a tracheotomy and extracted a peach pit to revive the patient.

But that was under Dr. Betz's supervision, while he stood beside her, assuring her she knew what to do.

Right now, she wasn't so certain.

She reached the group and shoved them aside. No time for proprieties right now. Kneeling beside the child, she did a quick visual assessment. Lips, blue. Eyes—rolled back in his head. Hands—cold and clammy.

She bent and laid her ear against his chest, not even giving herself the benefit of the stethoscope. Heartbeat faint and irregular, but still there.

She softly slapped his cheeks, first one, then the other, while calling his name. "Caleb. Caleb, can you hear me?"

When he didn't respond, she pinched the skin on the back of his hand. Then dug her finger into the space between his thumb and forefinger. Still nothing. Finally, she clenched her fist and ground her knuckles into his breastbone. He groaned but remained inert.

She looked around, finally landing on his father. "Tell me what happened."

"He was sitting here, working on a piece of leather. We were baling hay. The wind picked up. He said he couldn't breathe. By the time I got to him, he'd fallen to the ground. Unconscious. Like you see him now."

She nodded. "Looks like an asthmatic attack." Using her elbow, she gestured to her bag. "In there, you'll find a bottle marked BELLADONNA. Pour a capful of the liquid into his mouth as I hold him up."

Seth did as instructed, and she lifted the limp child and pried open his mouth. His father dribbled the milky liquid onto his son's tongue. As the child swallowed, Tessa whispered encouragement into the boy's ear until the cap was empty.

She laid him down again and repeated her efforts to rouse him. Not until she pressed her knuckles into his chest bone did he respond by pushing her hand away. "He's come around. Let's get him home and into his bed." She looked up when footsteps neared. "Hello, Melody."

The young woman, her cheeks pink from her exertion, stared down at Caleb. "Oh, Seth. I'm so sorry. Is he—"

Seth stood. "No. Tes—Nurse Mayer was able to help him."

Melody turned on her. "Oh you were, were you?" She pointed at the child who remained limp. "He doesn't look much like it." She glared at the men gathered. "Perhaps she doesn't know as much as she thinks she does."

Seth laid a hand on her forearm. "Melody, please don't—"

Melody covered his hand with hers. "Don't you see what she's doing, Seth? She's trying to divide our colony."

Tessa stared. Had she heard correctly? She stepped forward. "That's not true. I—"

Melody snatched the bottle from Seth's grip. "Belladonna? That's poison. It could kill him."

Tessa pried the medicine from her fingers. "Not when used properly." She pointed to the child. "Which I did. Or he would be dead now."

Seth gasped. "Nurse Mayer."

His reproof pierced her heart, and she stooped to return the container to her bag. "Take him home. I believe the dust and pollen in this field brought on this attack."

But Melody wasn't done. She pointed at her. "Nonsense. Coming in here, teaching things from the outside world that don't apply here. Our tradition says that sickness is caused by sin." She peered at Seth. "Perhaps something his mother did?"

Seth stepped back as though she'd physically struck

70

him. His mouth opened and closed a couple of times, but no sound came out. Then his chin dropped to his chest, and he led the way across the field toward his house.

Melody's cheeks paled then blazed again. She whirled to face Tessa. "You may try to worm your way into his heart and our lives, but you will never succeed." She stepped closer. "Never. Do you understand?"

A drop of spittle landed on Tessa's cheek like venom from a snake, burning her skin. She forced herself to remain still. To not react. In her experience, not engaging with another's vile behavior was the quickest path to the other looking foolish to onlookers and themselves.

A long moment of silence hung between them. Finally, one of the Brothers muttered instructions, and two men picked up the boy between them and followed his father.

Tessa snapped her bag shut and walked in the opposite direction. She had rounds to complete and patients to visit before the midday meal. She'd make certain to dine at a different kitchen than where Seth and Melody usually ate. There were several to choose from in High Amana. She didn't need the grief.

And she surely had no reason to indulge the woman's accusations. Because, in fact, it was obvious to her—and hopefully to the others as well—that the only person intent on division was Melody herself.

* * *

By late afternoon, Seth was beyond frustration.

Caleb still hadn't regained full consciousness. Hadn't opened those beautiful green eyes and recognized his father. Hadn't uttered a single intelligible word. Nothing but the occasional muttering, groan, or moan.

Would his son ever wake up? How long could he exist in this state? Why hadn't Nurse Mayer's medicine worked?

Was it because he lacked faith?

He cradled his injured hand against his chest as he paced the floor. What if Caleb slipped away as his wife had done? Would he bury his boy beside his mother? Two lives, snatched away far too young.

He paused at the foot of the bed and gripped the iron bedstead with his left hand. No. He would not permit it. He stared at Caleb, willing a toe to wriggle. A finger to move. Eyes to open.

When that didn't happen, he sank to the floor, eyes closed. A weight heavy enough to crush his chest, to smash him into the floor, to kill him, pressed on him. Like giant hands constricting his breath. He opened his eyes, surprised he and Caleb were alone in the room. No boulder across his body. No world resting on his shoulders.

He listened. Silence in the house. And outside. Melody had left about an hour before when he refused her admittance to the boy's room. Her pleading and whining hadn't moved him, and while he tried to be polite, judging by her stomping footsteps as she left, she wasn't well pleased with him at the moment.

He would have to apologize and assuage any unpleasant feelings between them. Even though he didn't like her reaction to Nurse Mayer, didn't appreciate the tine smile he'd noted when she asked if Caleb were dead, and didn't agree with her accusations against his dead wife, what choice did he have? He'd more or less been ordered to court the woman. To go against the instructions of the elders would bring more grief not only to him but also to his son.

He would do anything to make Caleb well. To make his life easier. To leave him a legacy of faith and family.

Even up to and including marrying Melody.

The lump in his throat constricted his breathing, and he panted as he considered his options. Nurse Mayer operated with assurance and expertise. He had no reason to believe she had anything but her patient's best interests at heart. On the other hand, he knew the dangers of Belladonna, deadly nightshade.

Surely she'd not thought to rid herself of a rival for his own heart?

No, he'd not believe that of her.

No matter what Melody shouted.

No matter what his heart whispered.

* * *

Tessa rubbed her temple where a headache had appeared about eight hours prior and hadn't eased since. She turned up the wick on her oil lantern and set her medical journal before her. Perhaps she could find answers between these pages.

The day had been long and stressful, not eased by the glances from others in Amana as she continued her rounds or as she ate midday meal with them. Word spread quickly, because by the time she reached Homestead just before the dinner meal, she encountered the same looks.

Had she really done her best?

Was her best good enough?

She flipped through the pages until coming to the section she sought. *On Asthma: Its Pathology and Treatment.* Reprinted from its original publication date of a number of years earlier, the discourse by Dr. Henry Salter of England had quickly made the rounds in America.

She ran her finger down the page. Medical experts proved that asthmatic attacks could be induced by various activities, including intense exercise, cold air, and irritants such as dust, pollen, chemicals, and animal dander. Her identification at the scene of the incident agreed. Too much dust and pollen had inflamed the boy's chest and sinuses, blocking his airways, and preventing him from drawing sufficient breath for consciousness. The belladonna, suggested as a way to calm the individual's breathing, place them into a deep sleep, and address the inflammation, seemed her best course of action.

But what next? She couldn't keep the boy sedated. And she couldn't restrict him to his home or encase him in a world where these irritants didn't exist in one form or another.

Having inherited this breathing difficulty from his mother, who died of the same affliction, provided little hope of the child growing out of the disease, as she'd heard others did. And she doubted that either Caleb or his father wanted a life of invalidism for him.

But she had no other answers.

And apparently, neither did Dr. Salter.

She closed the journal. Dear Dr. Betz, her mentor and wholehearted supporter of her desire to become a doctor, gifted her with a subscription last year. Such a precious man, who also bequeathed her the medical textbook he so cherished. And the other provision that brought her here, to Amana.

She sighed. Dr. Betz, determined to know for certain whether her interest in medicine was a passing one, invited her to come alongside him and apprentice in his small town practice. When he saw her calling genuine, he paid for her to attend the Female Medical College of Pennsylvania. But the next year, in 1866, her parents died in the cholera outbreak. Unable to function, she'd returned home. And when the dear doctor passed away soon after, a personal gift of money enabled her to complete her nursing credentials.

And now here she was. In over her head with a case that stymied her. No, Caleb was more than that.

And if she had to stay up all night reading, she'd come up with a solution to save him.

And herself.

* * *

The town clock gonged midnight. Seth raised his head and stared out the window, bleary eyes struggling to focus. In the bed beside him, his son lay still and pale, almost invisible against the sheets.

Seth stood and stretched. The hardback chair was of little comfort, and while he had slept, wasn't refreshed. Tomorrow would be another long day. Work to do. Expectations to meet.

How would he cope?

His eyes roamed the room, so familiar to him. How many hours had he and Anna spent, standing in the doorway, watching their son sleep? Not enough. And how many times had she tucked him into bed? Not nearly enough.

How many more days would he have with his boy? With the only part of Anna he had left? Never enough, not even if he had eternity.

His gaze landed on a needlework sample hanging over the bed. One his wife lovingly crafted while she carried their son in her womb.

Her favorite verse from the Bible: Now faith is the substance of things hoped for, the evidence of things not seen.

At the time, he'd thought it appropriate as God knit their child together in the secret place. As Caleb was fearfully and wonderfully made, in accord with their Lord's promises.

But couldn't God have given them a son free of this asthma? Why did others have children who could run and play in dust and dirt, and never so much as a sneeze out of them? Why did Anna herself, so beautiful yet so frail, suffer from that same affliction?

He turned his eyes to the ceiling. Was it too much for God to heal her? Or their son? Was this one thing He would not do because of sin in his life? Perhaps Melody's accusation was simply directed at the wrong person.

He fell to his knees, hands clasped and head bowed on the edge of his son's bed. His *dying* son's bed. And he cried out to the One Who could fix all this. If He wanted to. "God, I don't deserve anything You might choose to do for me. I've been disobedient in my thoughts and actions toward the woman You would have me marry. Please forgive me. Please don't punish my son for what I've done."

He raised his head. Had he felt movement? He watched for a moment, but seeing nothing, continued, the need to unburden his heart threatening to explode from within. "God, I'm sorry. I promise that I will take the first steps to court Melody. To treat her right. To love her the way she deserves to be loved. To provide for my family, and to put Anna from my heart. It's not fair to Melody to compare them."

Caleb gasped, then sucked in a deep breath.

Seth looked up. His son's lips were no longer blue.

His toes wriggled once. Twice. Then his eyes opened. Those beautiful green eyes. And they fixed on him. And his boy smiled.

"Papa. I'm hungry."

Just like Lazarus coming out of the tomb.

Chapter 6

After spending a restless night watching over his son—whose miraculous recovery was beyond words—on Thursday morning, Seth pushed Caleb in his chair the short distance to the dining room.

Word quickly spread about the boy's health, and Brother Abram made an appearance to acknowledge the event.

His cheeks pink from being the center of attention, Caleb beamed at his father from across the room. Melody didn't appear—a headache, Sister Leeken, her mother, explained, as she shepherded her remaining children to the table.

Seth wasn't convinced by the accuracy of the diagnosis, and judging by the way the woman didn't meet his gaze, neither was she.

Still, he would rectify that immediately after the meal.

After Brother Abram completed the final *amen* to the morning prayers and headed for the door, Seth caught his attention. "Brother, I've come to a decision. I would much appreciate a short meeting with the elders after meal."

"I will arrange it."

Seth turned back to his fried potatoes, raisin bread, and coffee. Whether he'd not noticed it before because his mind was preoccupied, or because of his impending decision, he wasn't certain, but now the food sat like a bucket of mud in his stomach. He pushed his plate away. He could eat no more.

When the brother beside him cast him a glance, he exhaled and brought the food closer. Waste was a sin, one they could ill-afford in the colonies.

He would eat and do his duty.

Yet again.

After breakfast and dismissal, he waited for his son. Sister Leeken's oldest boy, a year or so younger than his older sister Melody and fast approaching marriageable age himself, pushed the chair outside.

Caleb smiled. "Papa, Sister Leeken has a chair she'd like me to re-cane. May I go with her to see it?"

"Yes, you may." Had God just provided another answer to an unspoken prayer about how to explain his need to meet with the elders again? And so soon after his previous summons? "I will linger here for a while, then pick you up on my way home." He tipped his hat to the woman. "Thank you."

A half-smile tickled her lips. Had she overheard his conversation with the elder? Did she know of his need for someone to watch his son for a few minutes? Perhaps she suspected the purpose of the meeting?

He headed toward the meeting hall. While his previous journey here was filled with questions because of his ignorance as to the reason for the summons, this time was different.

This time he knew the outcome.

God had made it very clear that marrying Melody was the right thing to do. Hadn't he proven it by healing his son? Almost before the words were out of his mouth.

No, this was the proper course of action. After all, he'd made an agreement with God.

Standing before the elders again—this time, he didn't even take the empty seat—Seth acknowledged that he'd prayed and that God had shown him marriage to Melody was His will.

When asked if certain of this direction, he nodded. "He has made it plain to me."

Brother Abram glanced around the circle. "Then let us pray together that this path is anointed by the Lord, and that it will prosper you and the colonies."

The six men bowed their heads with each elder taking a turn to thank God for making His way known to them.

Finally, at the *amen*, Seth raised his head. "Thank

you for your time, Brothers."

He turned and left the hall, closing the door behind him.

The thud of the solid wooden door echoed the pounding of his heart.

As though the entryway to happiness and love had slammed shut.

* * *

Tessa's path to her afternoon appointments in Middle Amana took her through High Amana. As she passed Seth's house, she caught sight of Caleb in his chair, sitting under the shade of a cottonwood. In his hands he held a piece of canework.

Her heart leapt into her throat at the sight. Of course, several in Upper South Amana and West Amana mentioned they'd heard of his recovery, but none had details beyond that single observation. In all honesty, she expected him to still be weak and immobile and in bed. But this—

She trotted down the path, waving and calling to him. "Caleb. You're looking well." When she reached his side, she noted cheeks pink with fresh air, not fever. "May I listen to your chest?"

"Oh, Nurse Tessa. I'm so glad to see you." He unbuttoned his shirt to allow her access. "You cured me. Papa said you gave me medicine, and I slept all night. And I woke up asking for food." Then he held up his project. "I'm repairing this for Sister Leeken."

At the mention of Melody's family name, her hands shook. She drew two breaths, forcing her shoulders to relax. She must not let the woman irritate her. She must be the better person in this affair.

Focusing on her patient, she placed the stethoscope against his skin and listened then raised her head. "I can't hear if you keep chattering like a squirrel."

He clapped a hand over his mouth and giggled, but allowed her to complete her examination. "Am I all healed?"

She sensed his question went beyond this most recent attack, but she had no way of predicting the future. "Compared to yesterday, you are right as rain."

He giggled again, his little-boy laugh infectious as it wrapped strings as strong as steel around her heart and soul. If she could spend the rest of her life with this child, she'd die a fortunate woman.

She straightened and returned her instrument to her bag. She had no right to even think such a thing. Caleb wasn't her son. And if Melody had her way, she'd have little access to him.

No, she was better off staying away as much as possible.

"Nurse Tessa, are you here to talk to my papa?"

Yes.

No.

"I have other patients to see. Who are really and truly sick. Not hale and hearty like you." She smiled and waved her goodbyes. Spending more time now would only wound her heart further. "But I will check on you again soon."

Caleb returned to his work, and she left the light of her day behind as she continued her trek to her next patient. And the next. She considered her situation. Did the boy sense how much she cared for him? Did his father know of her growing attachment? And if so, what did he think? She was putting herself in a precarious situation, one where her heart was certain to be shattered if he—if he—no, she would not allow herself to visit those black caves in her mind.

Caleb would live a long, joyful life. He would certainly outlive her. He had to. He was all his father had.

Except that soon Mr. Seibel might have a new wife. And more children. Perhaps, like Job in the Bible, his life would be returned to him twice over.

But while the Bible never mentioned it, she often wondered if the book's namesake ever thought of his first family, even—or perhaps, especially—when surrounded by his second.

Could the love of a life ever be replaced by another?

Might a shattered heart be healed by another? A second chance at love?

If so, perhaps there was still hope for her.

Just not with Caleb or his father.

* * *

Brother Leeken lounged on a rock by the river. He gestured to the water with his chin. "My Melody says you and her spend time here. Walking. Talking."

"I brought my son here two evenings ago. She joined us." No point giving him the wrong idea, that he'd begun courting his daughter prior to asking permission. Such things simply weren't done in Amana. "The reason I asked you here—"

Mr. Leeken shoved his hands into his pockets, his portly belly making him look like a woman about to give birth. "'Spect I know why."

"You do?" Perhaps it was best to let him speak. His own mouth was so dry he couldn't. "Please apprise me of your thoughts."

"You're here to ask to court Melody."

There. The words were out in the open. Words he wasn't certain he could have uttered. At least, not so succinctly. He'd surely have beaten around the bush, speaking superfluous words about his need for a wife. His son's desire for a mother. The benefits of marriage. And all the time making the arrangement sound like excellent business sense.

That wasn't how this was supposed to be. It hadn't been when he'd spoken to Anna's father. Then he'd easily spewed on for minutes on end about their love for each other, his delight in her as a friend and helpmeet, their dreams for the future. How many children they wanted. How marriage would enable them both to fulfill God's plan for their lives individually, as a couple, as parents, and corporately in the colonies.

In those regards, however, this time around he lacked the words.

If Brother Leeken noticed, he made no mention. Instead, he chose this time to ramble on, somewhat incoherently, about how Melody excelled at various household chores, including cooking, baking, sewing, cleaning, and keeping a kitchen garden. According to him, she learned everything from her mother.

He patted his substantial girth. "And as you can see, I haven't missed many meals."

Sister Leeken, as it happened, used to be a Küchebaas before her increasingly growing family demanded more of her time at home. And Seth also knew on good authority that Melody's work ethic perhaps mirrored her father's, whose bad back kept him from doing much more than producing more Leeken offspring. Neither she nor her father had held any position longer than a few months in as long as Seth could recall.

No, he suspected his work load, rather than decreasing upon his marriage, would grow. He'd be taking on a strong-willed, recalcitrant, bone-lazy child.

Still, he kept a smile pasted on his face as Melody's father extolled her non-existent qualities. Not once did the man ask if he loved her.

That wasn't high on the man's list of requirement for a potential husband.

When Brother Leeken concluded by saying that once Melody wed, he and his wife could move the two youngest out of their own marriage bed, Seth's hopes for the revelation of at least one redeeming feature plummeted.

Leeken wanted the girl gone to make room.

Still, he'd promised God that if He healed his son, he'd court and wed Melody.

And everybody knew what happened to those who broke covenant with God.

Bad things.

Really bad things.

* * *

Upon leaving her final patient of the day, Tessa considered her next stop. Ideally, she'd head toward her own home. Enjoy the dinner meal. Collect her clean clothes at the communal laundry. Relax over a medical book or a small needlework project until time to retire. To do that, she'd turn left.

Or she could return home the long way around. Past High Amana. Past Caleb's house. For that, a right-hand turn.

Left or right? Both would bring her to the same place ultimately.

But one would perhaps inject a little joy along the way.

Or heartbreak.

What if she observed Mr. Seibel and Melody walking along, arm in arm? Whispering by the river?

Or kissing under a tree?

Yes, she'd heard the gossip, although none of those sharing the news would call it such. Word spread quickly in a place where newspapers were few and far between.

Seth Seibel spoke with Brother Leeken today.

There was no doubt in anybody's mind what—or rather whom—was the topic of that conversation.

So why torture herself?

She waffled with her thoughts all the way back along the road and down the main street of High Amana. She nodded to several residents she met, but none stopped to engage her in small talk. Still the mood seemed lighter, perhaps because of the boy's recovery.

Tessa paused opposite Caleb's house. Through the window, she observed the child and his father sitting at a table. The child's head bowed over some papers, and a pencil suggested he was catching up on his schoolwork. Mr. Seibel sat opposite, a book in his uninjured hand, the other cradled against his chest.

She smiled. While he might appear to be reading, he'd not turned a page while she stood here. Perhaps his thoughts were elsewhere. Pondering a problem. Questioning a quandary. Seeking a solution.

She inhaled the scents of wood smoke, cut hay, and farm animals. Perhaps the cows mentioned in a previous conversation? An owl hooted from a nearby tree, and she turned to locate the bird. Yellow eyes stared back at her, but apart from that, the animal's feathers served as the perfect camouflage.

She stole a final glance back at the domestic scene inside the house. Seth's sharp turn of his head alerted her to a problem. He flung the book aside and rounded the table where Caleb slumped, the pencil crooked in his grip.

Not again.

She trotted across the road and hesitated at the front door. Should she knock? No time. She entered and turned right into the living area. "Caleb."

Mr. Seibel looked up. "He was fine. Working on his school work. Then he coughed. His eyes fluttered. And he fainted."

She set her bag down and glanced around. "Douse the fire. Perhaps a back draft brought smoke into the room."

He nodded. "I'd noticed that but thought little of it. I thought his fit of yesterday was brought on by hay and dust."

"It likely was. But now that his lungs and trachea are tender, any petty thing might set him off."

She opened her bag and dug through its contents. Belladonna worked yesterday. Perhaps again today. She hesitated. In such a small child, poisoning was highly possible, particularly with two doses so close together. But what else? Castor oil, calomel, rhubarb—no. These were all for common ailments like constipation, indigestion, and diarrhea.

What had she read about last night in the article by

Dr. Salter? No, not there. In the textbook. Other non-traditional remedies. Dare she try one?

She propped the boy up, and his head lolled onto her shoulder as though entreating her to help. She pressed her ear to his chest. He was still breathing, although his lungs sounded like he was drowning in mucous. Scratchy, wheezy, growly breaths. Panting like he'd run a mile.

Which, if she didn't soon act, he never would.

"Quick. Put on the coffee pot. Boil it strong and hot."

While Mr. Seibel hurried to follow her instructions, she pulled out the extractor used to suction mucus from the mouth and nose of a newborn. Laying Caleb's head back, she inserted the tubing and pumped the bulb, drawing fluid from his nose and the back of his throat. With little other choice, she dumped two biscuits from a plate in the center of the table then emptied the extractor in it. She repeated this several times until the boy coughed and opened his eyes. Her joy was short-lived, however, because they closed again.

She shook his shoulder and pinched the tender skin on the underside of his tricep, and he roused again. When his father brought the coffee, she doused it with several spoonfuls of sugar but withheld the milk he offered. "Sometimes milk creates mucous, and he has more than he needs right now."

With Mr. Seibel's help, she woke Caleb enough to sip the coffee. At first he grimaced, but as he gained

90

strength, he sipped more. "Get another, Mr. Seibel. Plenty of strong hot coffee."

As the man refilled the cup, he paused. "What does it do?"

"Doctors aren't sure. But anecdotal evidence—" She paused at his furrowed brow. "That means, stories from patients and doctors outside of research. We can't necessarily verify that coffee is a solution, since perhaps the amount of sugar is the actual answer. Or the kind of coffee. How strong the brew. Things of that sort that would be controlled in true research."

He returned with the cup. "Already added the sugar."

She held the cup for the boy to sip. "As I was saying, anecdotal evidence suggests the caffeine reduces the amount of mucus produces, while also invigorating the body and increasing blood pressure, body temperature, and heart rate. All of which are stifled by an asthmatic attack."

Color returned to the child's cheeks, and he sat up and set the cup on the table. When he saw the plate of fluids, he grimaced. "Was that inside me?"

Mr. Seibel patted his son's head. "Yes, it was."

"Oh, just wait until I tell the boys at school tomorrow."

His father chuckled. "And just what makes you think you'll be going anywhere? I'm sure Nurse Mayer will say you need o rest."

She pulled the boy closer with one arm. Nothing

91

too affectionate. But surely permissible in this situation. "If he feels well enough to go to school tomorrow, he should go. The teacher will alert you if he needs to return home." She peered into Seth's eyes. "But stay in during play break. No dust for you for a few days. Promise?"

"Cross my heart and hope to—"

She planted a finger across his mouth. "We'll have none of that talk here. This is a day to rejoice and thank God, don't you think?"

The boy nodded. "And you, Nurse Tessa." He wrapped his arms around her neck and pulled her close. "*Ich liebe dich.*"

I love you.

Tears blurred her vision at his innocent words. How her heart ached to hear those words spoken by him.

And by another.

Chapter 7

The next day, Tessa left Homestead after breakfast to visit several patients in Middle Amana. As she walked, she considered all that had happened in the few days since her arrival. While folks nodded to her, nobody stopped to engage in conversation. Meals were always the most painful. She was accustomed to chattering with her fellow nursing students at table. They had precious little time to relax between classes, clinics, studies, and extra-curricular work such as research or their chosen specialty.

Her path took her past several houses on the outskirts of Amana, and she noted quilts hanging on the fences. Perhaps that was something she could take on to keep her hands—and her mind—occupied.

She followed the trail around Lilly Pond to Middle Amana. Today her patient list included two young first-time mothers, a child with a case of poison ivy, and an older man with an abscess on his foot that resisted

93

treatment.

She sighed, but not in frustration. She loved her work. Perhaps more than if she'd finished medical school. Nursing enabled her to treat her patients on a personal level, to get involved in their lives, if only for a short while. Doctors—or the ones she'd met—tended to be more clinical. Determine the cause, find the cure or treatment, and on to the next one.

At least in the case of the Amana Colonies, where she lived and worked, she had the opportunity to become acquainted with each patient on a personal level.

Such as Caleb. Twice now she'd been able to intervene in an asthmatic attack and bring the child around. Twice she'd seen medicine at its best. And not because of her or her expertise, although her specialized training in breathing ailments certainly helped.

She checked her visitation list for the day as she neared her initial patient's home. Sarah Hollipeter, age sixteen. Eight months into her first pregnancy. Planned to deliver with a midwife's help. A wise choice. No complications. Healthy and hardy. According to the few notes she had, still up with the sun and working all day.

She slowed at the walkway to the house and eased open the gate which screamed on rusty hinges. The amount of rain throughout the year rusted metal and warped boards with a vengeance, as though trying to obliterate both. She held the gate so it didn't slam, petted a black and white kitten that bounded over and swatted at her skirt, then

94

raised a hand to knock.

She hesitated when a familiar woman's voice sifted around the door.

"Oh, I've met her. She seems capable enough."

Melody.

Another woman. Perhaps Sarah? "Do you think she knows enough about babies?"

A chuckle. "From this side of the sheets, perhaps."

"Oh, is she not married, then?"

"I doubt she's ever had a man of her own."

Both women giggled as heat rushed up Tessa's neck. How dare they gossip about her behind her back? She would march in there and—and what? Admit she'd eavesdropped on their conversation? It was true what her mother often told her: listen at keyholes, and you'll hear something you wished you hadn't.

What to do? She glanced around. Nobody out this morning.

Footsteps neared from inside. "I must be off."

Melody again.

"I hear you've set your cap for that Seth Seibel."

"Yes. He spoke with Father yesterday. It's all arranged. We're officially stepping out together." A moan. "I hope he isn't one of those who believes in a long courtship and engagement. I am ready to be out of my family's house. Imagine sharing my bed with only one other person. What a treat that will be."

"And I imagine cooking and cleaning for but three

95

instead of more than a dozen would be a blessing, too."

"Perhaps there will only be two of us soon."

Tessa stifled a gasp. What was the woman implying?

"Oh, you don't think the lad will survive?"

"He's been sickly. And if he takes a turn for the worse, I won't know what to do. Seth is usually in a field or off on other business."

"Pray it isn't so."

"No, pray the Lord has His will. The mite suffers so. Is unhappy. Brooding. He'd be better off in heaven with his mother."

The footsteps paused on the other side of the door.

Tessa turned and hurried back the path, stepping outside the gate. She'd pretend she just arrived. They'd never know what wickedness she'd overheard.

The door opened, and Melody stood facing Sarah. "I don't like children. I think I've been responsible for my own brothers and sisters for so long that I'll enjoy married life without them for a while."

Sarah, standing just past the woman, formed an O with her mouth. "You know a way to prevent this, you mean?" She patted her protruding belly. "You must share with me. I'm thinking one is plenty, but my man wants a brood."

Melody nodded. "My grandmother told me about herbs and potions."

A lump the size of a goose egg rose in Tessa's

throat at the implications of her words. She was aware of those same treatments, often used after it was too late, often killing both mothers and babes.

Did Seth know of Melody's plans? Surely not. Why would he marry a woman determined to see his son die so young? Would she hurry along the process? Feign ignorance and bat her eyelashes when it happened?

And if she truly disliked children, why agree to marry a man with a child? Perhaps so when the boy died from her negligence, she'd be the center of attention and sympathy as the woman who took on another's sickly child to raise as her own.

Tessa gripped her bag in one hand and the fence in the other as her world swayed—nay, rocked—around her.

Who could she tell?

And who would they believe, when Melody denied that she meant what she said?

* * *

"But Seth, you know we'll marry. Why wait?"

Despite Melody's pleading tone, Seth held his ground, glad Caleb was well enough to attend school today and wasn't nearby to overhear their conversation. If he gave in to her pleading and whining now, she'd know how to defeat him every time they disagreed. He stabbed a bundle of straw and plopped it into the wagon. "Posting banns is serious. Once done, they are almost impossible to withdraw. Your father agreed we could court. We should do that for a while."

97

She jutted out her bottom lip. "Do you think you'll change your mind and not marry me?"

Images of Brother Abram's stern countenance filled his mind. "No. I will not." He tossed her a half-smile to soften his words and her temper. "But maybe you will. Perhaps your head will be turned by a man not mere years younger than your father. And one with a son to boot."

The beginnings of her smile slipped away. Was it the mention of her father?

Or his son?

No, he'd seen her with Caleb. Always doting, as his own mother would have been. Solicitous toward him. Praising him for accomplishments. Insisting he eat all his food.

He jabbed the pitchfork into the next stack and continued his work. He couldn't—and indeed, wouldn't—permit her to distract him from his duties. The town depended on all the workers doing their bit for its success. Not that Melody concerned herself with that, at least, not if he believed half what he heard about her work ethic.

Or lack of.

What was he getting himself into?

"But Seth, if you don't post the banns, people will talk about us behind our backs."

He grunted, and a bead of sweat rolled off the end of his nose, disappearing into the next forkful of hay. Which is exactly where he wished he could go, too. He straightened and locked gazes. He must make her understand the seriousness of his pledge without succumbing to her womanly wiles. "We will court. That's what I asked your father permission to do."

She stomped a foot. "But for how long?"

How long could he put her off?

"For at least a month."

He turned his back to her. Perhaps she'd understand this conversation was over.

But when she appeared in his vision again, with her arms locked around his neck and her lips searching for his, he saw he was wrong.

She wouldn't give up—or give in—easily.

She pulled his mouth down to hers, twining her fingers painfully in his hair. Scratching at his neck. Pressing her body—

He disentangled her from him and set her at arm's length, his cheeks flaming. He glanced around. A couple of the other field workers smirked and stared. No doubt word would be around all seven colonies by supper tonight. Suitably embellished with each retelling.

"Don't ever do that again."

She slapped his face. Twice. Hard.

He clasped his clenched fists to his side. He would not strike her, although this seemed to be her goal. He would not let her win.

Freezing in place, he glared. "If you don't want to court me, that's fine. But expect me at your house after evening meal with the intention of walking out with you."

He leaned closer and lowered his voice. "But if you ever try anything like that again, I will have the elders declare you a wanton woman. I'm sure I'll have no trouble finding witnesses, and I'll be free of my pledge. Do you understand me?"

Her nostrils flared and her pupils widened to darken her pale blue eyes. She stood rigid for several long moments before pasting on an insincere smile and bobbing her head. "See you tonight, *dear* Seth."

She turned and flounced her way toward the road, swaying her hips more than needed. The two closest workers leered, and one planted his hands on his hips and mimicked her motions.

Did the woman have no sense of propriety? Perhaps being raised in an extensive family left little room for privacy or modesty.

He exhaled and returned to his work. He'd won this battle, but feared not the war.

At least, not yet.

* * *

On her way home to freshen up before the evening meal, Tessa stopped in at the Widow Walter's home. Just to check on her.

The older woman invited her to join her on the front porch. "Sit a mite. You look worn out."

Tessa sank into the thick cushion on the matched rocker. "It's been a long day."

"I think I feel strong enough to attend the

100

communal meal tonight. Besides, *Zipporiesalaat* is on the menu on Friday evenings."

Dandelion salad.

One of her favorites, too.

"You won't wear yourself out?"

"My mama used to say it's better to wear out than rust out." A chuckle akin to a cackle slipped from the older woman's lips. "And I'm prepared to meet my Creator whenever He's ready for me." She closed her eyes and rested her head back on the chair. "Looking forward to seeing my husband Otto."

Yes, the widow had lived a good, long life. She had more laugh lines than worry wrinkles. She was comfortable, not in any pain. Tessa could pray for nothing better for any of her patients.

Particularly for Caleb. To know the boy would grow up, marry, have children, see his grandchildren—now that would be heaven on earth.

Not something she could look forward to for herself.

Mutter Agnes cleared her throat. "The first time we met, I perceived you are carrying a world of hurt. Why don't you cut it in half right now and share it with me?"

Tessa considered the woman's words. Could she trust her not to spread her burden? If she couldn't, then she dared not ask for advice on the other millstone she carried around her neck.

She exhaled. "You are correct. About a trouble in

my past."

"I am all ears. Eyes not worth a fig, but the ears are one way. Into the head. No exit. So don't worry about me telling anybody else." She chuckled. "Nobody listens to me anyway."

"I was engaged to a man who promised to love me and care for me always. But when my parents died, leaving me practically penniless after their debts were paid, he broke off the wedding. Two days before the date. And then spread malicious lies to make himself look good. Calling my reputation into question."

Mrs. Walter gasped. "The treacherous lout." She leaned closer. "Good."

"How do you mean? I was left with nothing except a dream of finishing medical school. Then my mentor and benefactor died."

"But you became a nurse."

"Yes, he left me enough money to complete the three-month course."

"But you know far more than any ordinary graduate."

Tessa smiled. The woman saw much more than those with perfect vision. "I completed one year of medical school before dropping out. And I apprenticed for two years with the doctor beforehand. Plus, I love to read and learn new techniques."

Sister Walter smiled. "Thank you for trusting me enough to share." She peered at her through unseeing eyes.

"What else is on your mind, Child?"

Tessa shrugged. "Nothing serious."

"Harrumph. Serious enough to stop you in your tracks." She tapped her temple. "I'm old, but I'm not daft. A benefit of being my age is that people don't expect you to remember anything. So they tell me things, ask for my counsel, knowing it will never be repeated." She patted Tessa's hand. "Tell me."

"I overheard a conversation." When the widow smiled, she hurried to explain. "I didn't intend to listen. I was at a door, and they were on the other side."

"Were they talking about you?"

"Partly. But mostly it was what they said about another. Or rather, two others."

"Brother Seibel and his son were the subjects of this conversation?"

Could the woman read her mind? "Y-yes."

"Are you taking offense for them?"

Tessa thought a moment. Is that what this was about? "No. I'm afraid Caleb might be in danger."

"That dear, sweet boy? From what, other than this dreadful ailment that claimed his *mutter*?"

"The person I overheard said perhaps it would be better if the boy died."

"Better for who?"

"Everybody. But particularly for Mr. Seibel and—and this person."

Phrasing her sentences so she didn't give away the

103

speaker's identity was something she hadn't considered. But who this person was shouldn't make any difference in the wise widow's counsel.

Sister Walter nodded. "I sometimes think God allows the weak and infirm to survive to remind the rest of us how blessed we are to walk in health. And to give us a mission field to demonstrate our love for those lesser ones, just as He showed love and compassion to us when we didn't know Him."

"I hadn't thought of it that way, but it does make sense."

"Do you know God and His Son personally?"

"Oh, yes. From a young age. I strive to serve Him, although I fall woefully short many times."

A raspy chuckle came from the older woman. "We all do, child. We all do." She leaned forward again. "What do you think you should do about this overheard conversation?"

Tessa tied her fingers into knots in her lap. "I don't know. I worry that if I stay silent, this—this person will succeed in killing Caleb or allow him to die. And if that happens, and I knew about it beforehand, I would be just as guilty of murder. Morally and perhaps even legally."

The widow nodded. "There is that."

"But if I speak to Mr. Seibel, he may be angry that I got involved. He may not believe this person would say those things. Or act upon them."

"*Ja,* that is possible." Her sightless eyes gazed

beyond Tessa, seeing something she couldn't. "Which is your greater fear?"

"That Caleb will die at—at the hands of or because of the negligence of this person."

"Are you willing to risk your friendship with the boy's father to prevent that?"

An ache filled her chest at the thought of not being on speaking terms with Mr. Seibel. But compared to the searing pain at picturing Caleb in a coffin, it was nothing. "Yes. Because if this person spoke their true intentions, one or the other is bound to happen, isn't it?"

"I fear so, child."

"Do you think it's possible the person spoke out of boasting, or the heat of the moment?"

The widow shook her head. "The Bible says that out of the abundance of the heart, the mouth speaks." She sighed. "I don't know if she meant the words when she spoke them, but the devil will use them to direct her paths."

"Oh, surely not." Tessa paused. "You knew who I spoke of all along, didn't you?"

"There are few in these colonies I would credit with those words, but Melody Leeken is one of them."

"You mean there are others?"

"Perhaps none other than she who would act, but some believe infirmity is a punishment for sin."

"But they're wrong. Disease is caused by a breakdown in the body's ability to fight off the cause of the illness. Would they say your blindness was because of you sin?" She sat back in her chair and crossed her arms over her chest. "I don't believe it."

The elderly woman smiled. "If not my sin, then perhaps my husband's." She patted a Bible at her elbow. "It's an Old Testament teaching, where everything bad that occurred was related to sin. No, I believe we live under a New Covenant now, one covered by Jesus." She smiled and winked. "But don't tell anybody I said that. They might run me out of the colonies on a rail."

With that, Tessa stood. "I must get along home and change for supper. Shall I stop and we can walk together?"

"That would be very fine, child. Thank you." *Mutter* Agnes smiled. "I wonder if there is any *Obstkuchen* left from last night?"

The fruit pie, heavy with peaches and cinnamon, *was* delicious. "I could enjoy another slice, too. See you in a half hour or so."

As Tessa continued toward her permit house, the miles she'd walked and the patients she'd seen that day weighed heavily on her mind. Was illness caused by sin? Why would a loving God permit such a thing, particularly to those who trusted in His Son? Perhaps the cause wasn't a specific person or an individual sin. Maybe sin itself was the cause. The same sin that came into the world through Adam and Eve, and now infected every person. Which explained the need for a Savior.

But what should she now do? Speak to Mr. Seibel?

Wait and see what happened? From what Melody said, her marriage to Caleb's father was a forgone conclusion. Perhaps she should wait until the wedding was imminent? But wouldn't it be more difficult to break off the engagement at that point?

Oh, for the wisdom of Solomon.

* * *

In the communal kitchen in Homestead, Seth scanned the room for one familiar face. Nurse Mayer. At first, he didn't spot her, but after searching across the bowed heads, there she was. At a different table, seated beside Widow Walter.

He smiled, hoping to catch her eye. But she never opened them, at least, not during the seemingly interminable prayers offered by an elder. He groaned as the food cooled and the gravy congealed. If he were a *Bruderrath*, he'd change the rules so the food came from the warming ovens after the prayers were done.

Still, just seeing her—even from fifty feet away—cheered his heart.

Which was wrong, wasn't it? Surely Melody should be the one to bring that lightness and uplift him, not another. Not a woman he could never marry because she was of a different faith. Nurse Mayer had a career that might take her many places outside the Amana Colonies. She had no need—and perhaps no desire—for a ready-made family.

At the final amen, he caught her staring at him, and he looked away, guilty at his candid gaze. What would she think of him?

But when he looked up, she smiled. Tiny, fleeting, but still there.

He held up his bandaged hand and raised his eyebrows in a silent question.

She glanced from side to side, then passed a plate, before nodding.

The rest of the meal passed in a blur. Apart from potatoes and gravy, he had no recollection of what else he ate. When the elder announced the end of dinner, he stood and left the building, waiting for her under the tree.

She exited with the widow on her arm, and his heart plummeted. He'd quite overlooked the two might have come together. Then she spotted him and she waved. "Mr. Seibel, good evening."

He crossed the small grassy area and nodded to the two. "Sister Walter. Nurse Mayer. Good evening."

The widow held out her other arm. "Help this old woman home, children, then be off with you. I am too tired to entertain tonight."

Seth looped his arm through hers, feeling more bone than skin through her long-sleeved blouse. Such a charming dismissal. "Gladly, Sister."

Within minutes they'd traversed the short distance to the older woman's home. Seth waited on the porch while Nurse Mayer helped the widow into her bed.

He stood when she exited the house. "I hope you don't mind taking a look at this wound for me."

"Not at all. I am surprised to see you here without Caleb."

"He's with Melody in High Amana."

Did her cheeks pale, or was that the moonlight on her skin? Either way, the effect was most becoming.

Not wanting to start rumors or raise eyebrows, he refrained from offering her his arm. Now that he courted Melody, she was the only woman who should occupy that place, apart from assisting somebody like Widow Walter.

They reached the nurse's house in minutes, and he gestured to a chair on the porch. "I'll wait here."

She smiled as though appreciating his sense of propriety. "I'll bring some salve and clean bandage. And a bowl of water in case I need it."

She was as good as her word, and returned bearing a tray containing those items. She set the supplies on a small table between the two chairs, then sat. A tiny snip of the bandage released its lengths, and she eased off the last couple of rounds stuck to the cuts.

Her lips pursed and her brow pulled down. "I'll clean it again then apply more salve and a new wrapping."

He peered between her fingers that moved at lightning speed. "Everything look good?"

"Oh, yes. Healing splendidly."

However, her words didn't comport with her expression. Was she withholding unpleasant news?

He pulled his hand from her touch and rotated it. "Nothing infected?"

"No." She dipped the end of a cleaning cloth into the bowl of water then dabbed at the cuts. "Hopefully this won't hurt."

No, he didn't even feel it. What hurt was the change in her demeanor from the day before. Gone was the lighthearted banter. Questions about Caleb's progress. Which was strange in and of itself. Apart from the one inquiry as to his son's current whereabouts, she'd not mentioned the boy.

"Caleb sends his love."

Her head snapped up as her hands froze in mid-air. Then her shoulders slumped, and she continued her ministrations, applying salve, then wrapping his hand up past his wrist. She slit the end of the bandage and tied off the wrap.

Professionally, unchanged.

So why did the mere mention of his son's name bring such a vehement response?

He laid a hand on her forearm. "Are you doing well?"

She eased away from his touch. "Fine. I had a long day. I'm really tired."

Perhaps he could ease her burden. He smiled. "Forgive me for taking up your time."

She stood when he did. "Did you eat the evening meal in Homestead just to seek me out?" Her cheeks flushed. "I mean, to seek out my medical expertise?"

Honestly? No. He couldn't bear to watch Melody

across the hall, fluttering her eyelashes at him. He'd see her soon enough, once he returned to High Amana. And he would fulfill his word. They would walk together for an hour or so. But no more moonlit walks along the river. No more parking Caleb under a tree and wandering off, just the two of them. The woman mistook that location as an invitation for intimacy. When they wed was soon enough for that, as far as he was concerned.

So he pasted on another smile and told a small white lie. "Of course."

He'd told only a handful of untruthd in his entire life. His habit was to be honest, sometimes brutally so.

But tonight, the truth wouldn't come out.

Not only was he avoiding Melody, but his spirit screamed to see Nurse Mayer.

In his current situation, that was a truth best kept to himself.

Chapter 8

Saturday morning, the end of her first week in the Amana Colonies, and Tessa less certain today she'd heard God's call to this place than ever.

Except her doubts had little to do with her ability to hear the Lord's voice but instead was related to her struggles with the residents.

Last evening, while tending to Mr. Siebel's wounds, she wanted to speak to him about his intention of marrying Melody, and to warn him of her threats regarding his son. But she couldn't get the words past the lump in her throat.

In the end, she'd decided to sleep on the matter one more night.

Before bed, while reading her Bible, she came across a familiar verse, now seeing it in a fresh light: *Whether therefore ye eat, or drink, or whatsoever you do, do all to the glory of God.*

This particular passage was a foundational part of

her upbringing, always used to reinforce the concept that work was important and should be done joyfully, so that others looking on would see God at work in her.

However, in her current situation, she recognized a new application: When what she did was for God's glory, her labors were good and blessed.

So she'd fallen asleep with the words echoing in her heart and mind. And when she arose this morning, with Sister Walter's words in her ears, she made her decision. Her motivation wasn't to earn a place in Mr. Seibel's heart or life for herself. Her goal wasn't to stop him marrying. Or to work her way into Caleb's life.

No, she wanted to alert Mr. Seibel so he could keep an eye on Melody when she was around his son. To ensure she wouldn't—or couldn't—follow through on her threat.

If anything happened to Caleb, his father's heart would break.

And she didn't want that.

Directly after breakfast, she headed for High Amana, having rearranged her patient visit list for the day. She passed through Amana and Middle Amana, taking her time. The weather, as usual, was perfect, although the nights were cooler with a promise of frost to come. Doves cooed from the cool reaches of the trees lining the road, and swifts performed their acrobatics in search of a meal. A flock of starlings rose from a wheat field like a black blanket, twittering their presence.

Once she reached the colony limits, she checked

each field for sign of Mr. Seibel, but he wasn't to be seen. Perhaps he worked at home today.

She continued toward his house, eager to get this one task off her mind so she could concentrate on her patients. As she neared the communal kitchen he normally frequented, she debated whether a quick stop for a cup of water and a snack would be beneficial. Deciding it would, she crossed the street then entered the building.

The *Küchebaas* peeked out from the kitchen. "Can I help you?"

"Water, please. And perhaps a little something to eat?"

Asking for food was still foreign to her. However, she had no trouble getting used to not having to cook. She set her medical bag on the floor then sat to wait. Within a few minutes, the older woman returned with a cup, a pitcher of water, and a small bowl of peaches, which she placedon the table.

"Thank you." Tessa's mouth watered at the sight of the cool drink and the refreshing fruit. "This looks wonderful."

The kitchen manager slid onto the bench opposite her. "Don't rush. It's nice to have company to chat with. You're the new nurse?"

Her mouth full of peaches, Tessa nodded.

"I've heard wonderful things about your work. Several of our expectant mothers say you have a gentle way with them." She sniffed. "Not like the last one we had."

"I'm sorry if my sister nurses were unkind."

"Intimidated, I would say. A little afraid of us with our closed ways." She studied Tessa up and down. "But you fit right in."

"I was raised Mennonite, so I understand the Old Order ways."

"That makes a difference."

"Did you see Mister—Brother Seibel today?"

The woman's face lit up. "Yes, him and his little boy. Here as usual." Another sniff. "And that woman." She leaned closer. "I heard her saying he was courting her. Is that right?"

Heat ran up Tessa's cheeks. "Yes, I heard that as well. Not from either of them directly."

"I don't know what's gotten into that boy's head." She chuckled. "Anybody under the age of fifty is a child to me. Includes you." The kitchen boss stood. "Nice chatting with you. Will you be here for midday meal? I'm doing baked chicken. Dumpling soup. Carrots. Pickled beets."

"I will be here. *Spatzle* is one of my favorites." Tessa patted her stomach. "You're making me hungry already."

"See you then."

She picked up the tray and disappeared back into her work area, from which chopping sounds soon emanated, beating a curious cadence like a tribal song.

Tessa headed outside and paused at the unmistakable sound of metal on rock. She peered around the building at the garden.

And Mr. Seibel, jamming a shovel into a hole.

How serendipitous.

She rounded the building. "Good day."

He paused and turned, his brow pulled down. But when he saw her, the corners of his mouth reversed direction. He swabbed at his face with a kerchief tied around his neck, then propped his shovel against the fence. "Nurse Mayer. How nice to see you again."

Did he really mean that, or was he simply glad to take a break from his labors? Didn't matter which. Hopefully he remained as pleased after she said her piece.

She gestured toward two stumps in the shade of the kitchen. "Do you have a minute or two to sit?"

"Of course." He wiped his hands in his pants legs and removed his hat before peering into her eyes. "Is it Caleb?"

"Oh, goodness, no. So far as I know, he's fine. At school, right?"

"Yes. Six days a week. Gives parents the chance to work, provides discipline for the children so when they become adults, they are already accustomed to working as God did. Six days then resting on the Sabbath." He waited until she sat before perching on the stump. "So what can I do for you?"

She held his gaze. "I pray you will hear me out."

"Sounds serious."

"It is. I've carried a heavy burden for the past day

or so, trying to make certain that my actions are motivated by the best intentions."

He tossed her a half-smile. "I would never doubt that. Go ahead." He cupped his hands behind his ears. "I'm all ears."

She drew a deep breath. "Melody has told people that you and she are courting."

He squirmed. "True."

A strange reaction on his part, to be sure. Most men would puff out their chests and smile, wouldn't they, at the discussion of courtship and pending nuptials?

She pushed on. "I know you are fond of her, and that she seems solicitous of Caleb."

"I don't know what I would have done without her help over the past two years."

Oh, how to say what needed saying? Would her words sound as crazy to him as they first were to her? Should she take seriously a woman barely out of her teens, one accustomed to having her own way and shirking her duties with few consequences?

Oh, God, give me the words, or shut my mouth immediately.

Her shoulders slumped under the weight of her message. Best to just speak it and let God work it to good. "I overheard a conversation between Melody and another woman in which Melody declared she was marrying you to escape from the overcrowded conditions in her family's home. She said she didn't like children. Would look for— for ways to prevent pregnancy." She paused to draw a breath. Now for the most difficult and hurtful part. "And wouldn't be upset if something happened to Caleb so she wouldn't be burdened with him."

Mr. Seibel blinked several times, as though she'd thrown water at him. He remained rigid as a statue, apart from those eyes. Green, just like Caleb's. Oh, yes, she'd noticed. Green as a lush meadow after a rain.

Then he stood. No, really more like he unfolded himself from the stump and towered over her, his face contorted into a mask of pain. Of anguish.

Of horror.

* * *

Seth stared at her. Had she really uttered those words? Accusing his almost-betrothed of harming the love of his life? Of denying God's will when it came to their own children? That Melody had no affection for him whatsoever, but instead saw him as a means to an end?

He grunted as he paced. As for that last point, he could hold her to no higher standards than he held himself. He was not marrying because of any passion for the woman.

He promised to wed her only because the elders indicated their belief that this union was necessary for the benefit of the colony.

Seth faced the nurse, hands on his hips. "You said you overheard this conversation. How?"

Her cheeks flamed red. "I—I—uh—I was visiting a patient, and she was inside the house."

118

"And where were you?"

"At the front door."

"Eavesdropping?" He practically spit the word out. "What next? Listening in at windows? Reading her mail?"

"No, it wasn't like that. I—I—I hesitated when I heard voices. I didn't realize it was her until she mentioned you, and Caleb, and—and—"

He raised a hand to stop her words and excuses. "I've heard enough. And what you've said has confirmed what I must do."

"Please, Mr. Seibel—"

He shook his head. "No more words. I'll thank you to stay out of our lives from now on, apart from treating my son. And I will put as much distance as I can between us. You are intruding into matters that are none of your concern."

"But—"

"Excuse me. I have banns to prepare, which I'll post them on Monday. I can see Melody was correct. The sooner we're married, the better. Particularly to stop the whispering and gossiping tongues."

* * *

While Tessa's preference, following her discussion with Mr. Seibel, would have been to escape to her house and hide beneath the covers, she finished her patient rounds. Thankfully, nobody else in High Amana appeared to know anything about the topic, but the colony was abuzz with news of the impending banns. Apparently, once Melody learned of his decision, she told anybody and everybody.

At home that night, as she completed her patient charts in her notebook and looked up several ailments in her medical journal, she contemplated the mess she'd made. She'd told Mr. Seibel with the best of intentions, but still the matter had turned sour between them. He thought she was trying to stop the marriage for other reasons.

But what could they be? Surely not jealousy. She was certain she'd never indicated anything of the sort. Besides, she was not of the his sect, and marrying into the Amana Colony was not an option, so far as she understood. No, if an Amanite man fell in love with her, they'd have to leave.

She sighed and pushed her papers aside, then turned up the wick on her lantern. The only thing to do was to pray. Ask God for peace for her heart. And his. She ached because of the hurt she'd caused him. How could she have misunderstood God's direction? Did she not apply Widow Walter's advice properly?

Was it possible she had feelings for Mr. Seibel she didn't recognize? Is that why she felt compelled to tell him what she'd heard?

The look of disgust on his face this morning frightened her. Was that truly what he thought of her?

She opened her Bible once again to her reading from the previous evening. First Corinthians chapter one and verse thirty-one: *whether therefore ye eat, or drink, or whatsoever ye do, do all to the glory of God.*

Well, she'd done that, hadn't she?

She rubbed gritty eyes and looked back over the previous verses. *When you see a therefore, ask what the therefore is there for.* Isn't that what the senior elder in her church used to say?

She swallowed the lump that appeared earlier today and wouldn't go away, pushing it down into the deep recesses of her heart. These verses were about eating food sacrificed to idols, and that once sanctified, the food's origin was now blessed. But wait, a few verses further back was about believers being of one body because of the communion of Christ.

She sat back, hands clasped in her lap. Melody was a member of this community, as were Mr. Seibel and Caleb. And all the others, apart from herself and the few outsiders who lived and worked in the colonies.

Perhaps the problem wasn't Melody.

Maybe *she* was the problem.

She bowed her head and prayed, asking God to remove any sin of jealousy or anger or wicked thoughts. Then she prayed for peace for Mr. Seibel, for God to bless his union with Melody, and for Him to protect Caleb.

She jumped at a furious pounding on her door, then hurried to answer. A lad she didn't know stood there, out of breath.

"Come in, child." Perhaps one of her almost-due mothers? She bid him sit then fetched him a cup of water, which he drained thirstily. "What is it?"

"Mr. Seibel. Boy is sick. Not breathing. Come quick."

No. She glanced at the ceiling. Was this God's idea of a joke? To answer her prayer for health for Caleb by sending him into an asthmatic attack? And what of his father? The last thing he wanted right now was to see her.

But that wouldn't keep her from going. He'd sent for her, and she'd do what she could.

She shoved her article by Dr. Salter into her bag and followed the boy into the night. Struggling to keep him in sight, she stumbled over every rut and rock along the way, but finally the High Amana town limits came into view. Several residents stood outside their doors, lanterns held high to light her way. She nodded and smiled to each one until she came to the Leeken household.

Melody held no light. She exhibited no goodwill to the nurse who'd run the two or so miles from her own home. She glared as Tessa trotted past.

If looks could kill. . .

No, she'd not entertain thoughts like that tonight.

She had a life to save.

The front door of Mr. Seibel's house stood ajar, and Tessa slowed only long enough to not trip on the threshold. Up the stairs she raced, her medical bag beating against her leg. Her own lungs screamed for air, but she wouldn't slow until she reached her patient.

In his bed, Caleb lay, fists clenched and eyes wide as he struggled for breath. Mr. Seibel glanced up at her then turned back to his son.

A woman, seated on the opposite side, moved out of the way as Tessa entered. "It's okay, Caleb. The nurse is here." She smiled up at her. "I'm Sister Graumann. I live next door."

Caleb turned glazed eyes in her direction. His lips tried to form the words, but all that came out of his mouth was a long, drawn out wheeze.

Tessa sat on the now-vacant chair. "What happened?"

Mr. Seibel shook his head. "I don't know. He was fine until we arrived home. We'd stopped at Melody's—" He paused and searched her face as though seeking her approval for his actions before continuing. "He had several cookies she'd made, which he ate on the way home. Then he said he had a headache, and his cheeks were flushed. I thought he had a fever. Before I knew it, his breathing changed. It's like he can't draw air."

Tessa pulled her stethoscope from the bag, pulled down the covers, opened the child's shirt, and listened to his chest. Some air moved, but not enough. She repositioned the instrument further up his trachea. A lot of congestion blocked his breathing.

She extracted her day-surgery kit and spread it on the bed then selected a scalpel. She looked across at Mr. Seibel. "In my bag you'll find a glass tube. Please hold it for me."

He came around and pawed through the contents

of her kit before holding up what she needed.

She nodded. "Good. Give it to me when I ask for it." She splashed alcohol on Caleb's neck, then leaned over him, locking eyes with him. "Caleb, don't move. Trust me."

The boy gave a tiny nod, his eyes still wide.

She paused at a hand on her arm, then turned.

"What are you going to do?"

"It's called a tracheotomy. A small incision below his larynx so he can breathe. The tube will hold the hole open. Then, once he's recovered, I'll stitch the hole up and he'll breathe as before, through his nose."

Mr. Seibel nodded, and she proceeded. Caleb moaned once when she made the incision, but the brave boy remained still. She swabbed the blood which seeped from the wound with cotton. The trachea was a little more tough, and so she went carefully. Cutting too deeply could sever the delicate tissue and kill the boy where he lay.

Perspiration dribbled down her forehead and into her eyes, blurring her vision, but she persevered. She held out a hand, and Mr. Seibel placed the tube into her grip. She tucked the glass tube, about the same size as her small finger, into the hole.

At once, Caleb took a deep breath. His color changed from blue to red then to a normal pink. He relaxed, hands flat at his side. A couple of stitches, and the breathing tube was secure.

She sat back, hands shaking in her lap. That was close. Another minute or two, and she'd have lost the boy.

Mr. Seibel shook his head. "I don't understand. None of his other attacks were like this."

The answer lay in what happened the last few minutes of their walk home. "I think this was an allergic reaction. Up to this point, his asthma has responded to common causes such as hay and dust." She met his gaze, their previous encounter still foremost in her mind. "What was in the cookies?"

He shrugged. "I don't know. Flour. Butter. Sugar. The usual things." He crossed the room and returned with a half-eaten cookie. "Here it is."

She sniffed it. Amaretto. And a lot of it. And bits of almonds, too. "Has Caleb reacted to any tree nuts before?"

"Yes. When he was little, he broke out in hives after eating walnuts and almonds. I'm careful to make certain he doesn't eat them."

"This cookie is full of chopped almonds. And amaretto, which is a liqueur made from the nut."

He shook his head and paced the room. "No, that doesn't make sense. Melody knew about—" He stopped and stared at her then sank onto the bed. "Do you think she did this on purpose?"

"I'm not certain. All I recommend is that you keep an eye on her. It might have been an oversight."

Her assurances sounded flat and insincere to her own ears.

Did they sound the same to him?

* * *

Seth shifted in the hardback chair in his son's room in the early hours of the following morning. He wouldn't leave the child's side until this dreadful episode had passed. Nurse Mayer and the neighbor and her son had been gone for hours, but still he couldn't sleep.

His harsh words and quick dismissal of the nurse's concerns earlier that day flooded him with shame. Surely the source of her information—straight from the horse's mouth, as it were—should have been of paramount importance to him. Not the fact that she'd overheard something not intended for her ears.

Instead of listening and weighing the validity of her concerns—for there was no doubt in his mind that she believed what she'd heard—he'd jumped to conclusions.

Incorrect, as it seemed.

He stared at his son. Was this how Abraham felt as he led Isaac up the mountain in keeping with God's command to sacrifice his son? But God hadn't spoken to *him* personally about this matter. In fact, He'd been woefully quiet on all matters recently.

Except, of course, for prayers when Caleb suddenly fell ill. And then, like an angel of God, Nurse Mayer appeared. Efficient. Calm. Skilled. And forgiving.

He closed his eyes. "God, what are You doing? I ask for guidance and wisdom about marrying Melody, but you remain silent. I begged you to save Anna, but she died anyway. I've prayed for Caleb's healing, but nothing." He swallowed hard, struggling for words to express how he

126

felt. "Yet each time when Caleb is near death, I pray, and you answer immediately. I promise to marry Melody, and he is healed. Even temporarily is better than death. Is that what You require? For me to fulfill my vow?"

He waited in the quiet for a moment, ears straining to hear even a single syllable from his Creator. "Is that what this is about? But which one? I promised to love Anna until death. Now she's gone. I promised her I'd take care of our son. I've done my best. What other promises have I made?"

First love.

"Anna was the first love of my life."

Return.

"How can I?" He sat forward, elbows on his knees. "She's gone. There is nobody else." He straightened. "Nobody but You, that is. Is that what you mean? Return to my first love? Jesus?"

He stood and traversed the narrow room before returning to his chair, careful not to wake the child. "I prayed, and You answered. But it wasn't because I promised to wed Melody, was it? You answered because I trusted You would respond. You could do it. You were willing." He glanced at the ceiling, striving to see beyond the beams and boards. "Is that what this is about, God? Me trusting You?"

Suddenly everything was so clear in his mind. As vivid as if the words were written on the wall before him.

Trusting God wasn't about making deals and

127

bargains with Him.

No, to truly trust God meant he had nowhere else to turn. Nothing to offer in return.

Well, if that's what God wanted, he was just the man the Lord sought.

Chapter 9

Sunday morning brought the promise of not only a day of rest for the Sabbath, but also the opportunity to visit with other residents at the enormous meal served at the church. According to the chatter she'd heard, each community celebrated on the same schedule.

Caleb and Mr. Seibel likely wouldn't travel to Homestead today for dinner.

She sighed. Already she missed the boy.

Still, on the bright side, Tessa could meet many of those in Homestead she'd only seen on the streets or in the fields. With several communal kitchens, she'd not met those residents yet. And thankfully, most were healthy and didn't require her services. Without the church midday meal, she might never get to know them.

The warm weather invited her to dawdle on her way from breakfast to service, but the chiming bells called her to hurry. Punctuality was smiled upon, while even a minute late to any prescribed meeting was not.

She slipped into the last row of benches on the

women and children's side of the building, scooting to the middle so others didn't have to step over or around her. The preacher stepped to the front of the church where a lectern held a large Bible. He nodded to a man in the front row, who began singing the German lyrics to the old hymn from the *Psalter-Spiel* hymn book.

An elder gave announcements, including the reminder about the meal following service, and then the preacher stood to pray and give the sermon. All in German.

Tessa groaned. If she was to garner any benefit from her time in church, she'd need to brush up on her *Deutsche*. For today, she'd focus on picking out words she did understand, and perhaps seek Sister Walter's assistance with the rest.

She did, however, comprehend the scriptural reference: Exodus the twenty-third chapter, specifically verse nine. His message, about treating outsiders well, because once the Amanites were also outsiders, resonated with her. Perhaps the people of Homestead would take his words to heart in her regard. And maybe, just maybe, her goodwill would extend to all those in High Amana.

Two faces flashed across her mind: Mr. Seibel and Melody. He was so angry with her when she told him what she'd overheard, yet had sent for her when his son fell ill. This time, perhaps at the hand of the woman who drove a wedge between them.

Not that much was needed. Caleb's father no doubt thought of her little. After all, he was a man soon to be officially betrothed.

The rest of the service passed quickly, and just about the time her stomach announced it was ready to eat, the last *Amen* uttered and the back doors were flung open. Children raced outside, wriggling and squirming between the adults in their haste. Tessa smiled, wishing she were able to demonstrate her exuberance in the same fashion.

She shook hands with the preacher. "Thank you for the sermon. As an outsider, I appreciate the sentiment."

His gray eyes smiled at her. "You are settling in?"

"Yes, very much so."

He leaned closer. "We have kept you on your toes over the past week, have we not? Particularly young Caleb Seibel."

"You are correct. But he is a dear boy, and I don't mind tending to him."

He patted her arm. "Don't get too attached. I hear he is soon to have a new mama."

She swallowed back a lump and nodded, wishing her heart believed what her head spoke. "That is excellent news for him and for his father."

The next person in line edged forward, and she continued her trek outside, her appetite gone. Or quenched, perhaps, with the dose of humiliation she'd experienced at the preacher's words.

Nothing like being put in her place.

* * *

Seth wheeled Caleb out of church and toward home. He'd

already turned down several invitations to the church midday meal. The dark circles beneath his son's eyes and the high flush on his cheeks bespoke the fact that the boy needed to rest. They'd enjoyed a hearty breakfast, and could wait until evening meal to eat again.

Since he hadn't slept well the previous night, either, he relished a few hours of quiet time.

At footsteps coming up behind him, he slowed and turned.

Then groaned.

Then pasted on a smile. "Melody."

She looped an arm through his. "Seth, I thought we would eat together at the church?"

"Not today. I'm taking Caleb home for a nap."

She waved off his words. "He's too old." She pinched his son's upper arm, drawing a tiny grimace from the boy. "He's not a baby anymore. You shouldn't treat him like one."

"He almost died last night." A terrible thought struck him. Surely Melody hadn't purposely fed his son nuts, hoping he'd die? No, that was too awful to fathom. "Did you make the cookies you gave him?"

She glared. "I told you I did, didn't I? Are you calling me a liar?"

"No."

"Then why ask such a question?"

"There were nuts in them."

She stared at Caleb who cringed under her gaze.

132

"What tales have you been telling, boy?"

His son ducked his chin to his chest and gripped the arms of the chair.

Seth glanced between the two. What a strange reaction. While he suspected the boy didn't love Melody—or at least, didn't hold the same degree of affection he did for Nurse Mayer—he'd never seen him act with disrespect. To not reply when an adult asked a question was most unlike him.

He nudged Caleb's shoulder. "Answer Miss Melody, son."

"Nothin'."

For his normally effusive son, another strange response. He shrugged off his concerns. The boy was obviously exhausted.

"I apologize for my son. He isn't himself today."

She kept her eyes on the child. "Oh, I'd say he's exactly like usual." She sniffed. "At least with me."

"Perhaps we'll see you at supper." Seth straightened his back and pushed the chair away from her before she could stop him again. In fact, he shouldn't have paused in the first place. Getting Caleb home was his focus.

And finding out what bothered him.

At home, he carried the boy upstairs to his room. Sunshine poured in through the window, and the bedroom was warm and stuffy. He set Caleb on his bed then closed the curtains. Perching on the mattress, he helped him off with his shoes.

Then he turned his attention to the boy's shirt and undid the lace. "Let's make you more comfortable here."

Caleb pushed his hands aside. "I'm fine, Papa."

Seth laid the back of his hand on his son's forehead. "No, you're not. You're burning up. You'll cool down with—"

"No, Papa. Leave it."

Shyness or whatever he exhibited toward Melody was one thing. But disobedience was something completely foreign. Seth had never known him to act this way. What was going on here?

Seth worked at the lace and slid his son's shirt off over his head.

And gasped.

His arms were covered with bruises and marks. Scratches spaced like fingernails. Indentations made by a hard object. And yellow, blue, and purple contusions, denoting the fact that the cause was ongoing. Some recent, some several days old.

Caleb pulled his arms from his father's grip and struggled to regain his shirt.

Seth pointed to one near his elbow. "What happened?"

"Nothin'."

Harrumph. Same response he'd given Melody earlier. And was no more enlightening now than it was then.

"Something must have happened. Bruises don't

134

simply appear for no reason." He pulled the boy into his arms. At first, Caleb resisted, then he melted against his chest. "Did a boy at school bully you?"

"No."

"Maybe Miss Melody's younger brothers? They can be a rambunctious lot."

"No."

He held his son at arm's length and peered into his face. "Then who?" His mind scrambled to determine the source. Who else was he alone with in recent days? "Nurse Mayer?"

Caleb pounded his father's chest with his fists. "No, Papa. Not her. She likes me. And I love her." He sobbed, giant tears trickling down his still-flushed cheeks. "I wish she would be my new mama and not—"

He swallowed back a hiccup and clamped his mouth shut. Caleb filled in the silence.

Not Melody.

He massaged the child's shoulders, so thin and bony beneath his touch. "Did—did Miss Melody do this to you?"

Caleb's chin touched his chest.

"Please, son, tell me the truth. You won't get in trouble."

His son raised his head. "Not from you, but she said if I told you or anybody, she'd—she'd—"

"She'd do what?"

"Make sure I never told anybody else." He grabbed

his father's shirt and clung to him. "Oh, Papa, I've been so scared."

Seth patted the boy's back, careful not to inflict more pain on tender skin. "When does she do this?"

"While we eat meals, she pinches my arms. When she pushes my chair, she pokes me in the back with her knee. She twists my arms, and sometimes she slaps me. She hides a belt buckle in her hand." He showed them by cupping his hand. "It hurts, Papa. But if I cry, she does it again. Harder."

His heart ached for the torture his son had endured at the hands of a monster he'd promised to bring into their home. Why would a woman do such a thing? Anna had never raised her hand to their child, or any other, and neither had he.

And neither would Nurse Mayer..

He held him close. Why, oh why, did he compare Melody to the nurse so often?

And why, oh why, did she continually fall so miserably short?

* * *

Less than an hour later, and Tessa stood in Caleb's bedroom, checking the evidence of Melody's handiwork. She had no doubt the boy spoke the truth. He had no reason not to, at least in her estimation. And his story aligned perfectly with what she'd overheard the woman herself say.

She rubbed salve on the abrasions, then pulled a

136

peppermint stick from her bag. "This is very important, Caleb. You must have some of this every day for the next three days. Whenever you hurt, you may eat a little. Can you do that?"

The boy bit off a chunk to demonstrate. "I can, Nurse Tessa."

She patted his head. "Good. Now, your father and I must speak."

Seth stepped aside, and she led the way downstairs to the living area where they both sat. Where to begin?

She drew a breath. "He is telling the truth. Melody—or somebody—caused those bruises. Do you have any reason to disbelieve him?"

He clenched his hands into fists in his lap. "No. Caleb doesn't lie." His shoulders slumped. "I'm sorry I didn't believe you when you warned me. And now my son is paying the price."

Her heart ached for the man. "You are not to blame. This has been going on a long time. Months, perhaps."

"Why would she do it?"

Tessa shrugged. "Perhaps she was jealous of the attention you paid him. Perhaps she is simply mean. Some people get much pleasure inflicting pain on others."

"Please forgive me."

She offered him a smile. "There is nothing to forgive. I don't know if I'd have reacted differently were he my son and you brought me such a tale. After all, I'm a stranger in the colonies. You've known Melody for many years."

His brow pulled down. "But I guess I didn't really know her at all, did I?"

"Sometimes that happens."

"Well, I believe you now." He glanced up at the ceiling. "Can you stay with him? I must go to the elders and tell them I will not be posting the banns tomorrow. I don't know what they will say. A man is nothing without his word and his honor."

"Surely they wouldn't expect you to endanger your son now that you know what she's really like?"

He lifted one shoulder and let it drop. "I do not know. I've never known this to happen before. Just as in the Bible, we are almost as good as wed. Almost."

"Of course I'll stay here to keep an eye on him. Take as much time as you need. And I'll pray for you both as you go."

He drew a deep breath, stood, and clapped his hat on before striding out through the door. At the street, he waved to her, then headed to the meeting hall.

But what if the elders refused to release him from his betrothal? Could they force him to wed a woman who might harm—or even kill—his son? Surely not?

She sat back in her chair. He was off on his difficult errand, and now she must complete hers.

To pray for one she both feared and disliked—without condemning her.

138

Chapter 10

Tessa woke early the next morning, her head pounding in time with her heart. She'd slept fitfully, and several nightmares disturbed her rest. Weary the previous evening by the emotion of the day, she declined Mr. Seibel's invitation to stay and talk. However, he looked as exhausted as she felt, and seemed glad when she left, as evidenced by the fact he didn't offer tea or coffee.

As she dressed for the day and checked her medical kit, she pondered her future here. Yes, she loved her work. Yes, she adored Caleb. And his father was a likeable man and would make an exemplary husband for a lucky woman.

Her heart quickened. She'd seen the way he looked at her prior to her earth-shattering discussion about his intended. And perhaps even the way he'd acted yesterday as they shared the painful discovery of Melody's mistreatment of his son. Tender. Transparent.

She added another roll of gauze bandage and

topped off the bottle of alcohol as the church bell gonged the call to breakfast. Could Mr. Seibel and Melody reconcile? Once confronted with her actions, would the younger woman admit her wrong and mend her ways? Prove that she could be a good wife and mother? Were her actions the result of jealousy? Insecurity? Or some mental or physical infirmity?

She donned her nurse's cap and cape—the morning was chill with the first hint of frost in the air—and grabbed her medical kit. If Mr. Seibel married Melody, she wouldn't stand in the way of his happiness. If he wed another, her admiration for him and love of his son might cause problems. She could not avoid the father because of the son's medical condition. Plus, Caleb wouldn't understand why he couldn't see her as a friend.

No, the only thing for her to do was to leave the colonies. In time, the boy would forget her as he settled into family life with whomever his father married. And Mr. Seibel would have his hands full with a new life and, eventually, more children.

Her mind made up, a millstone lifted from her shoulders. She would meet with the elders at her first opportunity and tell them her decision.

Then Caleb's father would be free.

She covered the short distance to the *küche* and entered the communal dining room. Caleb waved to her from her usual place at the end of the bench.

She slipped in beside him. "What are you doing

here?"

"Papa said he had important business in Homestead." He pointed. "He's over there."

She turned, and sure enough, Mr. Seibel waved. She faced the boy again. "How are you?"

"Fine."

The elder leading prayer today cleared his throat. "Let us give thanks for this day and our food."

Tessa bowed her head as the colonists lifted their prayers in German, while she added hers silently in English.

God, help me make the right choices. And give Mr. Seibel peace that You will send another nurse to care for Caleb and the other residents. And please show me where You want me to serve You, which I will strive to do for the rest of my life. Amen.

Once the meal was done, Tessa pushed Caleb into the open area to meet his father.

"Thank you for watching him. I hope he wasn't any trouble."

She smiled. "None at all."

She froze at a familiar figure approaching.

Melody.

But rather than stopping, the younger woman strode past, chin high, eyes straight ahead.

But not before she threw a murderous glance in Tessa's direction. One that stabbed her heart and paralyzed her mind.

Another woman led *Mutter* Agnes toward them, depositing the dear widow beside her before moving a few feet off to join another conversation.

Sister Walter patted her arm. "Greetings. I hear there are murderous expressions in the air today."

"Pardon me?"

The elderly woman sniffed. "If looks could kill, she'd have slayed half the colony by now." She gripped the back of Caleb's chair. "Young fellow, how about you help me over to that bench by allowing me to lean on your *Rollstuhl*?"

"Yes, Sister Walter."

The boy assisted by turning the wheels, and together the two made it to the shade of a cottonwood in record time.

Mr. Seibel chuckled. "How do you think she knew I wanted to talk to you? Alone."

Her mouth went dry at his words, and her sweaty palm threatened to lose its grip on her bag. "I think mind reading comes with age."

"Then that's a skill I look forward to acquiring."

"You wanted to speak to me?"

"Yes. I talked to the elders last night. They agreed I couldn't put my son in danger." He chuckled. "Actually, I think they were more concerned that Melody could have a mental impairment, particularly after their comments to me about Anna's and Caleb's less-than-perfect health."

"Yes, mental illness is much more feared. We know so little, but there are medical professionals making progress in that area."

"I doubt Melody will ever benefit. More likely she'll be shut away from small children and will eventually be referred to as that batty *tante* in the attic."

As much as Tessa disliked the woman, hearing his words pained her. Nobody deserved that. "Perhaps she will overcome her compulsions."

"Her recovery will take a stronger man than me." He gazed over her shoulder then focused on her again. "I have something I must ask you."

Her breath caught in her throat.

Most women would cheer to hear those words from a man they admired.

Instead, she feared the choice she might be forced to make.

* * *

Seth drew a breath, certain his heart would explode and he'd collapse before he asked his question. He gripped her hand, noting how her nose flared and her eyes widened. "Please stay in Amana."

"I'm sorry. I've already made up my mind." She frowned. "How did you—"

How did he what? Know she was planning to leave? He didn't. Hadn't dreamt such a thing. And why? Why would she leave? How ironic that at first he didn't want her—or any nurse, that matter. And now he wanted her to stay. More than he'd wanted anything for a long time.

"Were you leaving?"

143

Her cheeks paled and her breathing quickened. She glanced toward Caleb and Sister Walter. "I—I—I felt it would be best."

"For whom? Caleb? The residents? You?"

She pulled her hand away. "For everybody concerned. Mostly you and Caleb. So you could move on, find the woman who would treat you both right."

"And if you are that woman?"

"I can't be. If we wed, you'd have to leave the colony. And I wouldn't do that to you."

"If God said you are to be my wife, would you stay?"

"He said that? To whom?"

"It doesn't matter. Do you seek to be obedient to God?"

"Of course." Her eyes flitted from side to side then fixed on his face. "I will pray about it. But I won't be the reason you and your son must leave the only life you know."

"You won't be."

She stepped back. "What are you talking about?"

"After I explained to the elders what Melody had done, they agreed they'd been hasty to suggest her as wife for me. They asked if I knew of another suitable woman. I gave them your name."

"My name? Whatever for?"

He took half a step toward her. "Ever since you arrived, I've done little but think about you. Every time I

144

tried to imagine what married life would be, your face was the one I saw. You love my son, that's obvious. You love the people. You are much admired and much needed."

"Marriage requires more than that."

"It does. And I want to give you more. You've stolen my heart. You fill my thoughts. Now all that remains is for you to prayerfully consider my request."

"I don't know."

"*Ich liebe dich.* I love you."

She sniffled, her eyes moist. "I lost my heart to you a long while back."

He chuckled. "Really? You put on a good show otherwise. When?"

"About the time your son professed his affection to me. I built walls around my heart to protect it from being hurt. Again."

This was news to him. "Again?"

She blushed. "Not here. When we can talk alone, I'll share the whole sordid story with you."

"Hmm, a woman of mystery. I like that."

Her brow pulled down. "But what of the elders?"

"They know of your background. The Mennonite Tradition is one close to our own. The only fault they found with you was your woeful lack of German. But they are willing to grant an exemption and permit you to join our order as my wife."

"Please say you will."

Seth smiled at his son's silent approach, and at

145

Nurse Mayer's response.

She bent to meet his gaze. "I don't know."

"Why not?"

"Will you be able to call me Mama instead of Nurse Tessa?"

The child wrapped his arms around her neck, almost pulling her off balance, as he planted little-boy kisses on her cheeks.

She scooped him into her arms, hugged him, then set him back in his chair. "Goodness, you are getting much too heavy to carry."

Seth smiled at the scene before him then pulled a piece of paper from his pocket. "Walk with me—may I call you Tessa?"

She laughed. "Yes, please, Seth."

His name rolled off her lips as though they'd known each other forever.

And by God's grace, they would.

He held out the notice. "Come with me. We have to post this."

She snatched at the sheet. "What is it?"

"Why, our banns, of course."

She peered up at him. "You were pretty certain of my response, weren't you?"

He looped his arm through hers as they headed for the community notice board. "Not at all, but the elders were. Seems they've had their eye on you for a while."

Epilogue
September 1869

Tessa drew a deep breath and gave a hard push. A searing pain across her abdomen heralded the imminent birth of her first child.

Something the size of a watermelon pushed through her insides. Would this child never be born?

"The head is out." The midwife patted her foot. "One more strong push, and you'll be done."

Panting first, a strong inhale, and she bore down. Pressure *down there*, then a tiny squeal, and the birthing assistant held the child aloft. "A girl. A perfect, beautiful girl."

The tiny thing wailed, announcing its appearance,

and Tessa sank back on the pillow. Within minutes, the infant lay on her chest, lips moving as though whispering secrets to her. The midwife discarded the afterbirth and, while the child cooed, washed Tessa tenderly from head to toe with warm water sprinkled with a liberal dose of rosehips.

Tessa pulled aside her nightdress and allowed the child to suckle until it fell asleep at her breast. Then she checked to ensure there were ten fingers and ten toes. The midwife was right. The little girl was perfect, right down to her button nose and reddish blonde hair.

Footsteps on the stairs heralded her husband's appearance.

And directly behind him, her son's.

Walking on his own.

Caleb experienced a miraculous recovery in the past year. His asthmatic attacks became less intense and further apart, until almost four months passed since the last. His strength returned, and now he was as sturdy as any boy his age.

It seemed that once Melody was out of their lives, the asthma followed. Those colonists who insisted the boy's sickness was caused by sin had to admit that it was neither Caleb's nor his parents' transgressions that stood at the root.

Both gathered around the bed, and she patted the mattress. "Sit, both of you." She held the baby to Seth. "Would you like to hold her? She's asleep, so don't wake her just yet."

The sight of this vigorous man cradling their child in his calloused hands sent shivers of delight through her. Was it but a year since they wed? Little more than that since they first met? Yet it seemed as though she'd lived here all her life.

After a minute or so, Seth handed the child over to her big brother. "Here, hold her head like this."

Caleb sighed. "I know, Papa. I've been watching the mothers in the colony."

And true enough. She had no worries. "He's the perfect big brother."

Caleb looked up. "What's her name?"

She smiled at the picture they made. "Annagrace. How does that sound?"

The boy stroked the baby's cheek. "Mama would be so pleased." He looked at them each in turn. "I have two mothers. One in heaven, and one here with me." He kissed his sister's forehead. "And now I have a little sister to look after." He smiled. "We should have many more of these, Papa. And little brothers, too."

His father laughed. "You won't say that when they take your pencil or make a mess on your shirt or want to tag along with you and the older boys."

Caleb handed the babe back to her. "I won't mind."

Tessa tucked the child against her side, longing for a few minutes to rest. "I don't think you will at that. And how lucky your brothers and sisters will be to have such a

149

healthy big brother looking out for them."

Seth gripped her free hand. "God has truly blessed our family." He sighed. "Last year, when we learned a nurse was assigned to our colonies, I wasn't in favor of your coming."

"Oh. Why?"

"I worried that folks would depend more on medicine than on God."

"So what's changed your mind?"

"When I learned you had studied breathing therapies. And I thanked God for sending someone to help my Caleb." He smiled at his son, his daughter, and then her. "But now I see you came in disguise."

"I did?"

"Yes. A nurse for Caleb was really an answer to prayer for me. To heal my wounded heart, and to let me see that God had never forgotten me. He wasn't done with me yet."

She leaned over and kissed him, full on the mouth, in front of their son, delighting when her big, strong husband blushed. "And He's not done with any of us yet."

Dear Readers, Thanks for reading my story. If you enjoyed it, please leave a review online wherever you usually do that.

And also, follow the other stories in the series. Here is Book 2, "Justice for Julia", about a doctor accused of malpractice in the death of a patient:
https://www.amazon.com/dp/B09H9RFQX1
And the rest of the Series:
https://www.amazon.com/dp/B094NS9VTJ

ABOUT THE AUTHOR

A hybrid author, Donna writes squeaky clean historical and contemporary suspense. She has been published more than 60 times in books; is a member of several writers groups; facilitates a critique group; teaches writing classes; and judges in writing contests. She loves history and research, traveling extensively for both, and is an avid oil painter. She is taking all the information she's learned along the way about the writing and publishing process, and is coaching committed career writers. Learn more at https://www.donnaschlachter.com/the-purpose-full-writer-coaching-programs Check out her coaching group on FB: https://www.facebook.com/groups/604220861766651

www.DonnaSchlachter.com Stay connected so you learn about new releases, preorders, and presales, as well as check out featured authors, book reviews, and a little corner of peace. Plus: Receive 2 free ebooks simply for signing up for our free newsletter!

www.DonnaSchlachter.com/blog

Facebook: www.Facebook.com/DonnaschlachterAuthor

Twitter: www.Twitter.com/DonnaSchlachter

Books: Amazon: http://amzn.to/2ci5Xqq

Bookbub: https://www.bookbub.com/authors/donna-schlachter

Goodreads: https://www.goodreads.com/search?utf8=%E2%9C%93&query=donna+schlachter

The Purpose-Full Writer: https://www.facebook.com/groups/604220861766651

Need a writing coach? https://www.donnaschlachter.com/the-purpose-full-writer-coaching-programs

www.ingramcontent.com/pod-product-compliance
Lightning Source LLC
Chambersburg PA
CBHW071525170626
46811CB00007B/2953